"I've changed."

"Have you?"

The two words whispered about inside Kate's head, unlocking doors she thought were secured forever. Her body reacted instantaneously to Ashley's tone, and Kate's nipples hardened beneath her thin T-shirt.

Ashley moved closer still, and she slowly reached out, her fingers running over Kate's arm with practiced ease. Kate swayed toward her, terrified and exhilarated by her body's arousal.

Visit

Bella Books

at

BellaBooks.com

or call our toll-free number

1-800-729-4992

GOLD FEVER

LYN DENISON

Bella
BOOKS

2005

Bella Books, Inc.
P.O. Box 10543
Tallahassee, FL 32302

First published 1998 by Naiad Press

Printed in the United States of America on acid-free paper
First Edition

Editor: Lila Empson
Cover designer: Sandy Knowles

ISBN 1-59493-039-2

For Glenda,
my Little Treasure.

And for my parents,
gone too soon.

About the Author

Lyn Denison was born in Brisbane, the capital of Queensland, Australia's Sunshine State. She was a librarian before she retired to become a fulltime writer. Lyn's partner is also a librarian, which only goes to prove that tidying books is not all that goes on between library shelves. Apart from writing, Lyn loves reading, talking about books, cross-stitching, genealogy and scrapbooking. She lives with her partner in a historic suburb a few kilometers from Brisbane's city center.

CHAPTER ONE

All Kate's instincts for self-preservation demanded she escape to the refuge of her office as quickly as she could. But she made herself walk slowly, casually carrying the newspaper. She opened the door and stepped inside. Thank God the blinds on the glass panel were closed. She desperately needed to be alone.

Quietly she closed the door behind her, and as the lock clicked into place she closed her eyes, letting out the breath that had caught painfully in her chest.

Somehow her shaky legs carried her across the small room, around behind her desk, and she thankfully sank down onto her chair. Only then did she unfold the local newspaper she'd carried with such outward nonchalance. She set the paper in front of her on top of the acquisitions lists she had been working on earlier in the day. Then she slowly turned to the short article her assistant had so innocently drawn her attention to ten long minutes ago.

It was an innocuous piece really, in what was little more than a light gossip column masquerading as social chitchat. Kate forced herself to read the words:

Mr. and Mrs. Bill Maclean of Water Street will be at home this weekend celebrating Mrs. Maclean's sixtieth birthday. Among those attending will be the couple's four children — local businessman Baden Maclean and his wife, Susan; Belinda (Maclean) and her husband, Patrick Harrison, and family from Tully; Timothy Maclean and his wife, Gail, from Townsville; and Ashley (Maclean) and her husband, Dr. Dean Andrews, and family from Melbourne. Other relatives and friends will travel from as far away as Adelaide to join the celebration. Patsy and Bill then leave for a second honeymoon, a two-week cruise in the South Pacific.

"Don't you live next door to the Macleans?" Ryan Marshall, Kate's part-time assistant, had asked just before the young man left work, and Kate had nodded vaguely.

"Sort of. My house backs onto their property." She paused, eyeing the newspaper in Ryan's hands. "Why?"

"Sounds like there'll be a big party in a couple of

2

weeks and, according to my elder brother, the Maclean boys had a reputation for partying, didn't they?" Ryan asked lightly. "Your best bet might be to go away for the weekend yourself. Otherwise, maybe join them. For Mrs. Maclean's birthday," he added when Kate frowned uncomprehendingly. "You could always just drop in to wish Mrs. Maclean a neighborly happy birthday."

Ryan grinned. "Here, you might as well have the paper. I've finished reading it." He handed Kate the newspaper, and she took it automatically. "By the way, did you get that fax this morning?"

"Fax?" Kate repeated, as the thought of the Macleans seemed to be obliterating all else from her mind.

"From our visiting author's agent," Ryan explained.

"Oh. That fax. Yes." Kate tried valiantly to concentrate on the conversation.

"We've never had an author visit the library before, have we?"

Kate shook her head. "Not since I've been here."

"I'm really excited about Leigh Mossman coming to the library, aren't you? I mean, her book was just great. We all read it at home, and Mum and my sisters said the book had a hero to die for."

Last week Leigh Mossman's agent had sent a fax suggesting the up-and-coming young writer attend a literary afternoon at Kate's library as well as doing a book signing at the local bookstore. It seemed Leigh Mossman had spent part of her childhood in Charters Towers and she intended to revisit the town during a short holiday at the end of the month.

"*Gold Fever* is the best book I've read in ages," Ryan continued enthusiastically. "Apart from the fact that it's set here in the Towers, it is a real romantic story that I reckon appeals to both men and women readers."

Ryan took his reading seriously, and usually Kate thoroughly enjoyed his youthful insights.

"Have you read it yet, Kate?" he asked her.

She shook her head. "No, not yet. But I guess I should before Leigh Mossman gets here."

"Well, don't start it late because it'll keep you up reading all night, I promise you," Ryan warned. "Strange that no one seems to have heard of this Leigh Mossman. It has to be a pseudonym. Unless she's a descendant of Jupiter Mossman who discovered the gold here. What do you reckon?"

"Probably would have mentioned that in the promos if she was," Kate suggested, and he nodded.

"I guess. Well, all will be revealed at the end of the month. See you tomorrow, boss lady." Ryan waved cheerfully as he left.

And Kate had to continue on as though nothing had happened. Until she'd finally made her escape to the solitude of her office.

Just drop in to wish Mrs. Maclean a neighborly happy birthday, Ryan had said. Kate could almost smile at that if it wasn't so painful. In reality Patsy Maclean would just as likely ask her to leave, Kate thought wryly.

Then again, perhaps not. Since her aunt had died, she and Patsy Maclean had exchanged hellos a couple of times when they passed in the street. Maybe Patsy had begun to forgive after ten long years of silent condemnation.

Yet in the beginning it had all been so different. Quite the opposite in fact. Patsy Maclean had become almost a second mother to the quiet and lonely child Kate had been. She had certainly been the only mother figure Kate had ever known. Her own mother, both parents in fact, had seemed so remote compared to Patsy and Bill Maclean.

Kate grimaced self-derisively. With the benefit of her twenty-eight years she could understand her parents a little better. They had been respected academics, dedicated to their profession, and they must have been more than a little taken aback when in their late thirties they produced a baby daughter.

Kate was ten years old when her parents were tragically killed, and once their house had been sold and monies paid there hadn't been enough left for the expensive boarding school Kate was attending. So she had then been dispatched to the care of her only living relative, her father's much older sister, an aunt she hadn't known existed.

Jane Ballantyne, a recently retired legal secretary, lived in the Ballantyne family home in Charters Towers, one thousand miles north of Brisbane.

To ten-year-old Kate, compared to her reserved parents and equally withdrawn aunt, the members of the Maclean family were like colorful creatures from another planet. And Ashley Maclean, well, Ashley was... The familiar pain clutched at Kate's heart.

She saw so clearly two ten-year-olds, one dark-haired and one fair, riding their bicycles at breakneck pace along a rough track through the eerie rubber vines. Then the same two youngsters were climbing a mullock heap in search of gold, thinking they'd discovered a mother lode until Ashley's brother Tim had patronizingly told them the shiny metal was simply fool's gold, glittering far more brightly than the real thing.

Sitting behind her desk, she rubbed her eyes as the memories of the day she first met Ashley rose before her as clearly and vividly as if they were etched indelibly on her mind. If? She grimaced derisively. There was no *if* about it. Everything to do with Ashley Maclean had been carefully saved on the videotape inside her to replay itself whenever she dropped her guard. Even after all these years.

When her parents died, Kate's whole life had changed. Her father had left Charters Towers, his birthplace, some twenty-five years earlier, and Kate hadn't ever heard him mention the town of his birth or his family. Later she learned he had cut all ties after an argument with his sister and hadn't contacted her in all that time.

To have an unknown aunt collect her from the airport in Townsville and drive her the eighty-four miles to what was to be her new home in the Towers had been indescribably terrifying for Kate.

And the dry, russet tones of the historic inland mining town had been almost foreign compared to the relative greens of suburban Brisbane. She remembered the way her heart had sunk inside her young chest as her silent gaze went from her tall, austere aunt to the large old colonial house perched on its thick wooden stumps.

In those days Kate knew an almost constant overwhelming need to escape. Not that she didn't have her

6

own room in her aunt's house, a much bigger room than she was used to, but the house always seemed filled with her aunt's abstemious presence.

She had been with Aunt Jane for less than a week when she got up the courage to go exploring and discovered a refuge at the corner of the long back garden. There she'd found a sanctuary.

A huge tamarind tree spread its branches over her aunt's yard, and about a third of the way up the trunk there was a platform of planks. Someone had built a tree house of sorts. Rough, irregular pieces of corrugated-iron sheet formed a roof, and a crude ladder leaned against the back of the tree trunk, reaching the first huge branch.

Kate couldn't see her aunt constructing the tree house, and as it was out of sight of the house her aunt probably didn't even know it was there. So who could have built it?

Kate had tested her weight on the ladder and found it sturdy and solid. She climbed upward onto the lowest branch and then found footholds to reach the platform. She sat down on a wooden packing case and found herself smiling for the first time in weeks.

This, she decided, would be her retreat. Here she could sit and read and surround herself with her own private piece of the world, or what was left of it after it had turned upside down on her.

She stood up and moved gingerly on the platform to test its sturdiness, but it seemed quite safe and secure. Clutching a branch, she peered through the leaves at glimpses of hot tropical cobalt-blue sky.

And then she heard the noise, the cries of children playing, of deeper adolescent voices teasing, of adult laughter. Standing on tiptoe she realized she could easily see over the high wooden fence into the property backing onto her aunt's.

There was a swimming pool, glittering in the sunshine, turquoise blue dotted with tanned and glistening bodies. Off to the side was a yellow slippery slide that fed into the pool, and there were screams of laughter as children shot down to splash into the water. In the heavy heat, just the sight of those bobbing bodies immersing in the water made Kate feel cooler.

There seemed to be people everywhere. Adults, teenagers, young children. Even a couple of dark, shaggy dogs ran about enjoying the games and constant movement. And on the roof of a garden shed just on the other side of the fence a tortoiseshell cat disdainfully cleaned its paws.

Kate could barely take it all in. The color. The incessant activity. The noise. Such bright, happy, joyful, laughter-laden noise.

She had never seen anything like it in her life, couldn't even begin to imagine being part of it.

She learned later that the Macleans often had an open-house barbecue and that members of their large group of family and friends attended. But that first day she remained secretly in the tree house and watched, totally enthralled, until dusk. Then the outside lights were switched on, and the party continued. Kate would have stayed longer observing that other world, but she knew that her aunt would be looking for her for dinner and that she'd come searching if she didn't find Kate in her room.

So Kate took to spending every afternoon in the tree house, reading and watching the family next door. She even thought she'd sorted them out.

A woman with short, curly dark hair and a stocky, sandy-haired man were obviously the parents. There were two tall teenagers, a boy and a girl, and a boy a little younger. And one young girl who looked to be around about Kate's own age.

The girl had long golden hair that flew about her head as she bounced and turned somersaults on her trampoline. Kate watched her the most. And wished she could change places with her, be part of that always active, vigorous, loving family.

But of course she knew that was a pipe dream. She sensed she wouldn't be able to play the role had it been offered to her. She had never run on the grass without her shoes and socks, never slid dangerously down a slippery slide to splash into the water, or soared fearlessly upward on a trampoline. She wasn't adventurous enough to even try. Yet how she wished she was.

One afternoon a few days later she was sitting in the tree house trying to read. All was quiet next door, so she decided the family must be out. Disappointedly she turned to her book, but it wasn't holding her attention.

For some reason she kept remembering the quiet, book-cluttered house in Brisbane. Her father working in his study, half glasses on the bridge of his nose. Her mother in her own study marking student papers. The secure solitude of her own small room. Now this different, but still silent, house here in Charters Towers. The different heat. The different smells. And the disconcerting thought of a different school after the holidays. And she felt unaccustomed tears build behind her eyes.

"Oh. You've found my spot."

The voice gave Kate such a fright she almost fell off the wooden fruit crate she'd been using as a seat. Embarrassed, she dashed at her damp eyes with the back of her hand.

"Sorry. Did I nearly scare you to death?" The child had a pair of arrestingly clear blue eyes, and they crinkled at the corners as she smiled.

Kate recognized the long golden hair and felt suddenly guilty about her daily spying. Her heartbeats thundered inside her. "This is private property," she heard herself say pompously, and she stood up and glared down at the other child.

"I know. But I sometimes sneak in here to get away from the boys." Her small nose wrinkled as she inclined her head in the direction of the wooden palings and the exciting world on the other side of the fence.

Kate remained gazing down at the owner of the blue eyes, and her heartbeats continued to hammer in her chest.

The other girl's grin widened, and she reached up and grabbed a branch overhead. In one lithe movement, she swung herself up onto the platform beside Kate.

Kate stepped backward, keeping her space, and somewhere in the region of her heart something funny, something very strange, clutched at her chest.

She blinked, unable to understand the feelings that rose inside her. Yet she somehow knew that before her stood the most beautiful girl she had ever seen.

Afterward Kate was always reminded of sunshine after rain when she thought of Ashley. Ashley with her wide and smiling mouth and her thick golden hair, the ends bleached a shade lighter by the sun. Her eyes were the bluest blue, and a trail of light freckles crossed the bridge of her nose. She was shorter than Kate was and not as thin.

This was the child of the flowing hair, the one who turned miraculous somersaults on the trampoline. She was part of the alienness of that world on the other side of the fence. And Kate didn't know what to say to her.

"You must be Miss Ballantyne's niece. We heard you were coming to stay with her."

Kate wondered who had told them. Somehow she couldn't see her aunt volunteering any information.

"I'm Ashley." The girl held out her hand, and Kate automatically reached across and nervously took it.

Warm fingers closed around hers, and she felt herself grow suddenly hot. She quickly pulled her hand away.

"Ashley Maclean, actually." The other girl smiled again. She put her fair head on one side and raised her eyebrows inquiringly. "So, what's your name?"

Kate hesitated a moment and glanced toward the house. Would her aunt want her to be talking to this child?

"No one can see us from either house," Ashley said lightly. "That's why I picked this spot to build my tree house."

"You made this?" Kate couldn't prevent herself from asking as she indicated the wooden platform.

"Yes. And it was pretty difficult, I can tell you. I always had to wait until Mum and Dad and Miss Ballantyne were all out in case they heard me. And of course I had to sneak Dad's hammer and nails and not get my brothers suspicious. If they knew, they'd have wanted the tree house for themselves. Brothers are the pits." She sighed. "Have you got any?"

"Any what?" Kate stammered.

"Brothers, silly."

"Oh. No. There's just me."

"Gee, you're really lucky." Ashley sighed again. "So, are you going to tell me your name or shall I guess?" She frowned and pursed her lips. "Mary Anne? Eloise?" She giggled. "I know. Susan!"

Kate shook her head slightly, her gaze drawn to the other girl's smiling mouth.

"No? Okay. How about Rebecca? Or maybe Jennifer? I've always loved that name. In fact, I would have preferred being called Jennifer."

In that moment Kate could almost wish that was her name. "It's Kate," she said flatly. "Katherine, really. But I've always been called Kate."

"Kate." Ashley Maclean's sunny voice said the name experimentally and Kate's young heart seemed to flip over in her chest. "Kate," Ashley repeated. "I really like that." Her blue eyes skimmed Kate's pale face, her nondescript light brown hair, her unremarkable gray eyes. "It suits you."

"It does?" Kate murmured before she could prevent herself, feeling herself blush crimson.

"Yes. It does." Ashley laughed and sat down, cross-legged, on the platform.

"Oh. Do you think so?" Kate asked uncertainly. "I've always thought Kate was sort of old-fashioned." She surprised herself by confiding.

"Why? Were you named after your mother or what?"

Kate shook her head and sat down on the box

12

again. "No. I guess my parents must have just liked the name."

"At least it's not a sissy name like mine." Ashley wrinkled her small nose as she leaned forward, elbows on her knees, chin resting in her hands.

The tree house was suddenly far too small, and Kate moved her box seat backward a fraction.

"Mum was reading *Gone with the Wind* when I was born," Ashley continued easily, "so I was going to be Ashley if I was a boy or a girl."

"I think it's a nice name," Kate said politely.

"Thanks." Ashley grimaced and changed position, resting back on her hands, bare feet out in front of her.

To Kate's consternation that brought the other girl closer to her, her legs almost touching Kate's. Kate moved surreptitiously to balance on the edge of the crate to put some space between them.

"No, don't move. There's plenty of room for both of us." Ashley grinned. "Although if we're going to share this spot we'll have to find another box, and we'd better renovate, add a board or two."

Kate glanced at the wooden boards as if she'd never seen them before, and Ashley laughed at her expression.

"My father's a builder, and I've been helping him and the boys for years. I'm almost an expert," she added jauntily. "So, what are you reading?" She reached across and took the book Kate still held in her hand. She turned the book over and glanced at the title before handing it back to Kate. "Not bad, is it?"

"You've read it?"

Ashley nodded. "At the beginning of the holidays. I

borrowed it from the library. Mum says if I'm not careful they'll have to operate to remove a book from my hand. I read a lot."

"I do too."

There was a moment's silence.

"I'm reading one of Mum's at the moment, and it's full of sex."

Kate stiffened and felt herself flush again. "Does your mother let you read her books?"

"Are you kidding? She'd have ten kittens if she knew. Belinda's read it, so I don't see why I can't."

"Who's Belinda?"

Ashley grimaced. "My older sister. She's nearly seventeen and really up herself." She wrinkled her nose again. "She's a pain in the neck. Always bossing me round. It's a relief to come in here. If it's not Mum or Belinda on my back, it's those rotten boys."

"How many brothers do you have?"

"Two. Baden's Belinda's twin, and then there's Timothy. He's nearly fourteen. They're all adolescents." Ashley rolled her eyes. "That's why you're lucky being an only child. It must be so peaceful," she finished with feeling.

Kate couldn't actually say. But she just couldn't imagine having brothers and sisters.

"So how long are you staying with Miss Ballantyne?"

A wave of the now familiar panic clutched at Kate and she swallowed. "I don't know. For, well, for a few years anyway." Until she was old enough to live on her own, she could have added, but didn't.

"A few years?" Ashley's dark brows rose in surprise. "I thought you might have just been here for the school holidays. Where are your parents then?"

Kate blinked, and Ashley raised her fine eyebrows again. "They're dead," Kate said at last, and the words seemed to hover over her, reverberate inside her, and it was all suddenly so painfully final. She swallowed but couldn't hold back the tears that filled her eyes and began to tumble down her cheeks. It had been eight long weeks since the funeral, and Kate hadn't cried. Until now.

"Gee, I'm sorry. I didn't mean to upset you," Ashley was saying, and then her warm arms were around Kate, burying Kate's face in the curve of Ashley's neck. Ashley smelled of sunshine and sweetness. Ashley's hand gently rubbed Kate's back, and Kate wept some more.

To this day she couldn't explain the reason for her raw sorrow. It wasn't as though she had been very close to her parents. Not like she later discovered Ashley was to her mother and father.

More often than not, Kate's parents were away and she was at boarding school. She barely saw them for a few weeks a year. And since she'd arrived to live with her aunt, her aunt hadn't even mentioned Kate's parents. Ten-year-old Ashley Maclean had been the first person to offer her the physical comfort of her young arms.

And at the time Kate knew she'd never forget the first time Ashley put her arms around her, the sensation of that closeness to Ashley, those few moments of suspended time when she was filled with the other girl's compassion, with the feel of her body, the heady scent of her skin.

Kate had drawn back and then the whole story had come tumbling out, about her parents' accident when they were combining a short holiday with her father's lecture tour. The bus in which they had been traveling in Mexico had slid over an embankment, and Richard and Margaret Ballantyne had been two of the twenty-five people killed. Kate had been at boarding school, and the headmistress had summoned her to tell her the news.

Sitting alone in her office eighteen years later, Kate rubbed at her aching eyes with her hand. With hindsight she knew she couldn't blame her teachers or the maiden aunt who had had a ten-year-old niece thrust upon her, for Kate knew she had been a solitary, self-possessed child. At least she'd appeared that way. Sent away to school as soon as she was old enough, it was a shell Kate had grown as some protection. But she'd never been like that with Ashley.

That moment on the platform of the tree house they later renovated together had been the beginning of their friendship, a friendship that had ended so agonizingly eight years later.

And Kate hadn't seen or heard from Ashley since that dreadful time. Not that she had expected to, not after the first long weeks of numbed disbelief. Many times Kate had started a letter only to tear it up before she could find the nerve to post it.

Now Ashley Maclean was coming home to the Towers. No, not Ashley Maclean. Ashley Andrews. And she was coming home with her husband.

16

CHAPTER TWO

Just at dusk Kate drew her car to a halt in the driveway of Rosemary's house and switched off the engine. Because she'd sat brooding over the Maclean family reunion, Kate was late leaving work so she'd had to race home to take a quick shower and change into comfortable jeans and a T-shirt.

She sighed, wishing now that she'd phoned Rosemary and cried off their Thursday night dinner. She felt tired and disoriented and wanted to be alone to think about the newspaper article and its ramifications.

Yet part of her acknowledged that spending the evening in her empty house wasn't such a good idea just at the moment. Being alone would only invite other memories she'd rather not dwell on tonight.

The porch light shone welcomingly in the fading light, and the door opened. Rosemary peered out, and Kate made herself climb from her Ford Laser.

"Thought I heard your car," Rosemary said lightly as Kate walked up the short flight of steps.

Kate managed a smile. "Sorry I'm a bit late."

"No worries." Rosemary closed the door behind Kate and reached out, pulling Kate into her arms. "This is always worth waiting for." She kissed Kate eagerly and ran her hands down Kate's back, cupping her buttocks, moving Kate closer until they were breast to breast, stomach to stomach, thigh to thigh.

Kate made herself relax into the other woman's body, responding despite herself to Rosemary's lingering kiss.

Rosemary murmured as she drew her mouth from Kate's. "You feel wonderful, but I guess we'd better save this for dessert, otherwise our dinner will be ruined."

"Can't have that," Kate agreed easily.

"Not after I've slaved over a hot stove for, oh, ages and ages." Rosemary reluctantly released Kate and led the way along the short hallway. "Feel like some wine?" she asked over her shoulder.

Kate nodded. "That'd be great." She followed Rosemary into the small, graciously decorated dining-cum-living room, her eyes moving over the other woman's slim contours.

Rosemary Greig was a slender redhead, and she moved with an efficiency that seemed to carry over into every facet of her life. She was an attractive woman on the right side of forty, and she'd moved to Charters Towers a couple of years ago to take up the position of personal secretary to the city's lord mayor.

"So. What's for dinner?" Kate forced herself to make an effort. She knew her blue mood had nothing to do with Rosemary. "It smells delicious."

Rosemary passed Kate a glass of wine. "Thai this week."

"You'll have to let me cook for you," Kate began, feeling guilty that Rosemary always made their meal.

"When my cookery course is finished. I told you I appreciate having someone to try out my newfound skills on." She set out warmed plates and began serving. "It's so much better when you have someone to cook for besides yourself."

Kate sipped her wine, savoring the cool liquid on her tongue. "You're enjoying this cookery course, aren't you?"

Rosemary nodded. "Very much." She walked around the breakfast bar with their meal. "Please to sit down, madame," she said with a flourish.

They sat companionably eating by candlelight, and Kate felt some of her tension leave her. Sitting at home brooding, she knew, would only have made her feel worse. And if Rosemary noticed Kate was a little quieter tonight than she usually was, she made no comment.

Now, pleasantly relaxed, she was even glad she'd come. Rosemary was an entertaining companion, and she regaled Kate with pithy stories of the other students in her cookery class. By now Kate felt she knew them all, and she found herself laughing easily at Rosemary's anecdotes.

After the meal Kate helped with the dishes, and then they moved back into the lounge, sitting side-by-side on the sofa.

"Want to watch TV?" Rosemary asked and then raised her eyebrows and twirled an imaginary mustache. "Or are you ready for dessert?"

"Oh, such subtlety." Kate laughed. "What a technique. Let's relax a little first." She rubbed her tummy. "The meal was delicious, and I think I've overindulged."

"You have no staying power," Rosemary teased as she curled up against Kate and linked her hand with Kate's. "You look tired and seem a bit preoccupied. Had a hard day at work?"

Kate sighed. "Just the usual. Oh, and we had a verification fax from the agent of that new author, Leigh Mossman. It's all set that Leigh Mossman will be here in a couple of weeks, so I must try to read her book before she arrives. I don't usually read historic novels, but Ryan says this one's fantastic."

"*Gold Fever*? It's not bad."

"You've read it?" Kate asked in surprise.

"Mmm." Rosemary nodded. "Just finished it. I bought it after you told me she was coming to the library. I know having it set in the Towers makes it all the more interesting, but apart from that it's a really good read. Do you know yet who this Leigh Mossman is? I mean, I presume she's an ex-local."

"No one seems to have heard of her."

Rosemary grinned. "Ah, a mystery woman. But it is pretty well written for a first book. I can see why it's doing so well."

"Everyone who's borrowed it from the library has

enjoyed it, so we should have a good turnout on the afternoon. I hope we do anyway, if only to silence Phillip." Kate pulled a face. "He suggested it might be a waste of money when I mentioned catering for the afternoon, just tea, coffee, and finger food."

Rosemary groaned. "What? Quibbling over a few sandwiches and some fancy cakes? Isn't he the end?"

Kate grinned. "We're going to make the sandwiches ourselves, and Ryan's mother's making some of her famous cakes and cookies. It's a labor of love by the sounds of it. The whole Marshall family loved the book."

"My sister said she saw Leigh Mossman on the *Midday Show* in Sydney a month or so ago. She said she was really nice. Of course, the fact that she's quite young, blond, and beautiful won't do anything to hinder her career."

"Oh dear. So cynical." Kate laughed, and Rosemary smiled too.

"You sound better than you did when you arrived," she said lightly. Kate shrugged.

"Guess I've simply had an off day."

"Phillip hasn't been trying to further his case by asking you out again, has he?"

"No. Thank heavens." Kate grinned. "But if he does, at least this time I'll be prepared. I certainly didn't even suspect he was interested in a social life so soon, let alone that he wanted me to share it with him. I mean, I don't even think his divorce is final yet."

"Pity he's so —" Rosemary paused, searching for a relevant adjective.

"Insipid?" Kate finished, and Rosemary nodded.

"That'll do." She glanced at Kate. "Didn't you say you've known him since schooldays? Was he always such a bore?"

"Pretty much so."

"So, has he been carrying a torch for you all these years."

Kate stiffened slightly. The conversation was getting a little too close to a truth Kate didn't want to explore just at the moment. It was all too raw even now, after ten long years. "Carrying a torch? I wouldn't say that," Kate said carefully.

"Well, I can understand it if he was," Rosemary said huskily and took Kate's chin in her fingers. "You're very attractive. You have poise. You're intelligent —"

"I have my own teeth," Kate put in dryly, and Rosemary laughed delightedly.

"Absolutely essential in a town clerk's wife."

"Oh, please." Kate groaned. "Don't even think along those lines."

"Well, you can't blame the guy. He's dull but not a fool. He knows every good man needs a good woman, and by all accounts his last one left a little to be desired. But you'd be ideal. You're well-known in the town. You don't have any ex-husbands or children in tow. And, as you so charmingly said, you have your own teeth. Perfect."

Kate laughed. "Except for one small point. I'm not interested."

"Well, two small points," Rosemary reminded. "One, you're not interested. Two, you prefer women. For which I'm most grateful."

Kate smiled and then sobered. "It all gets so complicated, doesn't it?"

"Sure does. Especially in a place like this where everyone knows everyone else's business."

"It's the double standard that has always irritated me. Have you noticed they just about expect a bit of heterosexual bed hopping and a dabble into adultery, but when it comes to homosexuality they purse their collective lips and turn all conservative and pious?"

"Absolutely." Rosemary grimaced. "And pity help a gay guy in this man's town. Ah, the patriarchy is alive and well in these parts and won't be taking kindly to a hint of lesbianism in any of its women either."

"You mean there are lesbians in town?" Kate asked with mock horror. Rosemary chuckled.

"So I've heard. Never seen any, mind. At least not doing it in the street and frightening the horses."

Kate joined in Rosemary's laughter and then sighed. "It's not easy, is it?"

"No, it's not. Which is why I find the suggestion that it's a choice to be gay so incredible. Who in their right mind would want to live their life in the proverbial closet if they had a choice?" Rosemary shook her head. "Anyway, let's get off that depressing subject. I can think of better ways to spend my time with you."

She slid her lips along Kate's jawline, and her teeth teased Kate's earlobe, her mouth settling in the curve of Kate's neck. "Mmm. You smell delicious."

"Sure that's not the leftover aroma of your delicious dinner?" Kate asked ironically.

Rosemary groaned. "Such a romantic!" She skidded soft kisses on Kate's tender skin.

A romantic, Kate's mind repeated. She had been in the beginning, when her love for Ashley had all but consumed her every waking minute. Kate forced her attention back to the here and now, and when Rosemary's lips nibbled on Kate's earlobe Kate turned her head, her own lips finding Rosemary's in a kiss that desperately sought to claim the present and blot out the past.

"Well," Rosemary laughed softly. "That response bodes well for what I have in mind." Her fingers slipped beneath Kate's T-shirt, her hands closing over the firmness of Kate's small breasts. Kate's breath expelled on a half moan as Rosemary grazed her thumbs over Kate's hardening nipples.

"Oh, yes," Rosemary murmured appreciatively, but when Kate went to unbutton Rosemary's blouse Rosemary stopped her. "No. Not yet," she said. "I want to concentrate on you first," she added huskily and lifted Kate's shirt up and over her head, tossing it onto the floor.

She unclasped Kate's bra and leaned forward, taking one hard nipple into her mouth, tormenting with the tip of her tongue, gently teasing with her teeth.

Kate arched in response, her hands clutching at the soft cushions of the lounge chair.

Rosemary tenderly pushed Kate sideways, laying her on the couch. She unzipped Kate's jeans, peeled them off, and slowly slid her fingers under the edge of Kate's underpants. Her fingers touched lightly, pulled back, touched again, and Kate's hips rose as her nerve endings tensed in anticipation. Rosemary slowly slid Kate's underpants downward, and Kate murmured appreciatively as the other woman's hands slid back up the length of Kate's leg.

Now Rosemary's fingers found the curls of dark

hair and slipped into the dampness within. Her long fingers filled Kate, her thumb circling Kate's clitoris, and Kate moaned. Kate's body tensed as Rosemary slowed and then quickened her pace, her lips raining soft kisses over Kate's flat stomach. Then her mouth replaced her thumb, and she used her lips and tongue to lift Kate higher until, with an assuaging cry, Kate crested and fell into a shuddering release.

"You are very talented," she said when she'd caught her breath.

Rosemary chuckled. "You're not so bad yourself." She took Kate's hand and drew her to her feet. "Let's get more comfortable, and you can return the favor."

Kate allowed Rosemary to lead her down the hallway into her bedroom. She quickly dispensed with Rosemary's clothes and lowered her body to Rosemary's. Afterward they lay side-by-side and watched the moonlight dance across the ceiling.

Kate turned her head to look at Rosemary. "When did you first know?"

"That I preferred women?" Rosemary laughed softly. "You or women in general?"

Kate pulled a face. "Women in general."

"I guess I always knew deep down. But I grew up in a town smaller than this one, and you know what small towns are like. The pressures to conform are so much greater than in the city. I even went so far as to marry my best friend's brother."

Kate raised her eyebrows in surprise. "You were married? I didn't know that."

Rosemary pulled a face. "It wasn't the highlight of my life. You see I really wanted to marry my best friend, not her brother."

Ashley's face, her laughing blue eyes, flashed into Kate's mind, and she had to push away painful memories. "Did you tell your best friend that?"

"No. Never." Rosemary looked away, seeing her own obviously disturbing demons.

"Do you still love her?" Kate asked softly, and Rosemary shrugged.

"Not really. There's been a lot of water under the bridge since then. I don't think she ever forgave me for divorcing Tom, but I thought I'd already ruined five years of his life. So I left it all behind me and headed for the anonymity of the big smoke. I found the clubs and haven't looked back. How about you?"

Kate shrugged. "I was about fifteen when I realized I loved women," she admitted carefully. *A woman*, she corrected to herself. "I had a couple of brief affairs when I was away at university but, well, it was and is too difficult."

"Especially so here in the old hometown," Rosemary finished and Kate nodded. "Funny we've never talked about this before, isn't it? I guess we never seem to get around to it."

"Food and sex." Kate raised her eyebrows. "Do you suppose our relationship is too shallow?"

Rosemary laughed and ran her hand up Kate's thigh and over her flat stomach, settling her fingers on the rise of her breast. "If it is I'll settle for shallow." She gazed into Kate's eyes. "For the time being anyway," she added softly, and Kate tried not to look guiltily away, feeling she was using Rosemary and not wanting to admit it to herself.

Rosemary raised herself on one elbow. "So what about you, Kate? What's your story? Was there ever anyone special?"

Kate had never spoken to anyone about Ashley, and she hesitated now.

"Ah." Rosemary gently touched Kate's lips with her finger. "Do I know this lucky woman?"

Kate shook her head. "No. It was a long time ago. We were both so young. Too young."

"But it still hurts."

"Perhaps a little." What an understatement, Kate derided herself. She was beginning to suspect it still hurt a lot.

"Tell me about it."

"Oh, I don't know. It wasn't anything startling. Happens all the time."

"That doesn't make it any less painful," Rosemary said gently.

"It was all such a mess," Kate said, her voice breaking unconsciously.

"Where is she now?"

"She moved down south."

"She 'done you wrong'?"

"Not exactly. As I said, we were both very young."

"And?"

Kate swallowed. "Her mother found us together." The familiar feeling of shame began to clutch at Kate, but she thrust it away. She had nothing to be ashamed about; she'd kept telling herself that. What was shameful about loving someone the way she'd loved Ashley?

"In flagrante delicto?"

"Oh, yes." Kate grimaced.

Rosemary groaned with feeling. "I see."

"We were in her room." Kate shook her head. "It wasn't much fun, I can tell you."

"I can imagine it wasn't. So what happened then?"

"Well, everything and nothing." Kate sighed. "Her mother went aggro, threatened to tell my aunt and her father." She shrugged. "Then she married her boyfriend and that was that."

"You mean they married her off?" Rosemary was incredulous.

"Not exactly." Kate swallowed. The truth of it still cut through her like a knife. "She chose to get married," she said flatly, and Rosemary was silent for long moments.

"Oh, Kate. I'm sorry. It must have been awful."

Kate shrugged. "As you said, there's been a lot of water under the bridge since then." She peered across at Rosemary's bedside clock radio. "What time is it?"

"Almost midnight." Rosemary sighed too. "Wish you didn't have to go. Why don't you stay?"

Kate pushed herself into a sitting position. "I wouldn't be able to sleep for fear I would sleep in."

"I really hate all this sneaking about," Rosemary grumbled. "We are consenting adults, after all." She pulled Kate back down across her. "You were fantastic tonight," she said and kissed Kate eagerly.

Kate kissed her back and gently drew away, that same surge of guilt clutching at her as the thought that she had been making love to a memory rose to taunt her. "I'd better go."

"I guess you'd better." Rosemary sighed. "Before I get other ideas," she added with a rueful smile.

Kate padded into the still lighted living room and retrieved her clothes. Rosemary joined her. She'd pulled on an oversize T-shirt and she followed Kate to the door.

"Thanks for dinner." Kate paused. "And for everything."

"The dinner was nothing. But everything was really something." Rosemary chuckled. "So, lunch on Tuesday?"

"Sure," Kate agreed.

Rosemary reached out and pulled Kate into her arms one last time before she opened the door for Kate to leave. Rosemary waved as Kate backed out of the driveway and headed for home.

There was barely a lighted window to be seen, and Kate wondered why she didn't just stay at Rosemary's for the night. It would be so much easier on both of them. To make love and then have to get dressed and go home seemed so sordid somehow. And she was twenty-eight years old, for heaven's sake. Who gave a damn what she did anyway?

Stifling a yawn, Kate shifted gears as she turned her car out of Rosemary's street. In actual fact, she frowned. She was worried this whole thing with Rosemary wasn't just a little dishonorable on her part. Oh, she liked Rosemary, and in the beginning it was a relief in itself to have someone to talk to, to dine with, somewhere to go. But she knew Rosemary deserved more than Kate could give her.

As the lord mayor's personal secretary Rosemary worked at the city hall, not far from the library, and they'd met when Rosemary came into the library to check on some historical facts for a leaflet her office was producing. It had been pure coincidence really.

Usually Rosemary's assistant would have come down to see Kate to check the research. He was off work sick, however, so Rosemary had walked down to the library herself. She'd stopped to chat and then returned next day to ask Kate to share lunch at a nearby café. Kate had been pleased to go. It had been a distraction when she had been feeling a little flat with her job.

Kate had applied for and got the position of city librarian three years earlier, not long after she'd returned to Charters Towers when her aunt was taken ill.

It wasn't that she didn't enjoy her job or that she didn't feel she had made her mark on the position. The library had a much more visible profile now that she had implemented her ideas. They had more displays, encouraged visits from local schools, and held a weekly storytelling session that was well supported.

It was simply that recently she'd felt just a little jaded and unsure of the direction of her future.

Now that her aunt had passed away, she really had no ties with the Towers. Did she want to remain here or move on to a bigger city and a more demanding position? So she'd been pleased to accept the distraction of Rosemary's invitation.

After that first lunch, Rosemary and Kate fell into the habit of lunching together a couple of times a week at a popular local café that served all natural fare, sandwiches and burgers, quiches and low-fat desserts, and Kate soon began to look forward to her hour break.

However, Kate certainly hadn't been looking for an affair. It was the furthest thing from her mind. But a couple of weeks later Rosemary had started her gourmet cookery course, and she'd asked Kate if she could try out her newfound skills on Kate. Kate agreed.

The first evening they'd enjoyed Rosemary's meal and retired to the living room with their coffee. Kate sat on the two-seater lounge chair, expecting Rosemary to sit opposite in a single matching chair. Instead Rosemary had sat down beside Kate and gently removed Kate's coffee cup from her hand.

Then she'd turned to Kate and kissed her. Kate had stiffened in shock. Until that moment she hadn't considered the possibility that Rosemary might be a lesbian. Their conversations had been very superficial, restricted to their respective jobs, their fellow staff members.

"Have I shocked you?" Rosemary asked.

"Well . . . yes," Kate acknowledged.

"Offended you?" Rosemary continued lightly enough, but Kate could see the flutter of the pulse at the base of her throat.

"No, I'm not offended," she said, trying to make a decision about where she should allow this to go. She had always kept that part of her life rigidly controlled, especially since her return to the Towers.

Rosemary picked up Kate's hand and held it lightly in hers. "Have I read you wrongly? Just say so if I have." Rosemary continued to look down at Kate's hand. "I don't want to spoil things between us, Kate, but I thought, well" — she shrugged — "I thought we might be like-minded."

Kate swallowed quickly. Was she that obvious? Surely not. She was so careful. The only thing she couldn't bring herself to do was date men. Not that that had been so difficult. Her tall, angular body, almost nonexistent figure, and unexceptional features didn't exactly have men lining up outside her door.

Rosemary sighed. "Look, Kate. It's okay. You don't have to say anything. Can I just ask you to forget this ever happened?"

Kate drew a steadying breath. "You didn't mis-

31

construe anything, Rosemary," she said softly. "I'm just a little taken aback. I didn't think I was that, well, visible."

"You're not. Believe me." Rosemary laughed quickly, obviously relieved. "I'm usually fairly accurate at picking up on it. I'm ten years older than you, so I've had a lot of practice. Oh, I didn't mean that I'd had a lot of partners." She grimaced. "I'd best stop while I'm ahead, hadn't I?"

"I think so." Kate smiled, and they sat looking at each other.

"So, do you find me absolutely repulsive?" Rosemary asked softly, and Kate shook her head, making a decision and leaning closer to kiss the other woman.

From that night six weeks ago, Rosemary had cooked dinner for them each Thursday night and they had eaten lunch together a couple of times a week.

Kate frowned as she drove into her carport beside the house. She suspected Rosemary was more involved in their relationship than she, Kate, was. And Kate knew she had known that for some time. She simply hadn't wanted to deal with it. She wasn't sure she wanted to examine her own feelings. Especially now that Ashley was coming home.

And how would that make a difference? she demanded of herself. What Ashley did had no bearing on her life and hadn't for ten years.

Oh, yes! A small voice inside her jeered her mercilessly. Writing off her feelings for Ashley had been so easy!

Stifling an urge to slam the car door with more force than was necessary, Kate restrained herself in deference to the lateness of the hour and strode purposefully around the house and up the wide front steps. What possible bearing could Ashley's return have on Kate's relationship with Rosemary? Ashley was coming home with her husband and, Kate reminded herself, she was definitely not coming home to see Kate. Ashley had made her choice years ago.

On Saturday afternoon Kate felt restless. She'd refused Rosemary's offer of a weekend away, and now she wished she'd accepted the other woman's invitation.

She'd used up some of her excess energy cleaning the house far more diligently than she usually did, and now she had to admit that there was nothing left to clean.

When her aunt died two years earlier and Kate had inherited the house, she'd had the bathroom and kitchen remodeled. Then she had repainted the rooms in lighter, far more pleasing colors.

The house was a large old Queenslander, distinctive in that it was built for the tropical climate. Up on stumps with a high-pitched roof it was surrounded by wide, cooling verandas. Inside it had high ceilings, VJ walls, and fretwork over the arched doorways.

Just lately Kate had realized she enjoyed the house's old-world ambience. And although Kate and her aunt had come to grudgingly enjoy each other's company, Kate realized she was beginning to like living here on her own. It was only on the occasions when old memories resurfaced that the buried loneliness crept out to taunt her.

Now, with all her chores completed, Kate prowled

around the house. Basically she knew what was wrong with her. The tree house was beckoning the way it used to do, and she told herself it was ridiculous to even contemplate going down to the backyard. All that was behind her. It was simply kid stuff and adolescent angst.

But she couldn't seem to settle to reading, and just after three o'clock she found herself walking down the back steps and moving toward the huge old tamarind tree. She broke off a tamarind and cracked open its pod, sucking on the sweet-sour flesh. An acquired taste, most people agreed, but Kate loved it and still made a drink from the tamarinds just the way her aunt had taught her.

Awkwardly Kate climbed the ladder, found the familiar foot-and handholds, and swung herself up onto the platform. She looked around, trying not to peer over the fence. Of course, it was a little more difficult now to see into the Macleans' yard as the leafy branches seemed to have grown thicker over the years. There was a silence to the house next door that told Kate the family was not at home, and with this realization some of the tension that had been holding her stiffly left her.

In the weeks after that dreadful confrontation with Ashley's mother and its aftermath, Kate had dogged the tree house in the hope that Ashley would change her mind. She dreamed they would run away together, go south to Brisbane, get jobs in the city, blend into its anonymity.

But Ashley's wedding day arrived without Kate so much as seeing the other girl. Kate had sat in the tree house in abject misery that day and counted the minutes. When it became obvious that Ashley wasn't going to join her, Kate had vowed to leave the town, never to have to set eyes on this special place again.

Of course she had returned when her aunt became ill, and once again this place had been a refuge when she could get a few moments away from caring for her aunt.

Over the years some of the planks had rotted, and Kate had had them replaced, unable to allow the tree house to just decay with age.

She gingerly sat down on the canvas deck chair, testing it with her weight. It remained steady, and she relaxed. She looked around her, feeling the intimacy of the seclusion seep into her. She could almost pretend she was a child again, then a shy adolescent. But there was no Ashley to climb up beside her, laugh with her, share secrets with her. Or make love with her.

Kate felt again the heavy sense of loving and losing and then the pain of betrayal. She sighed. This wasn't playing by the rules. She'd made a pact with herself not to sit in the tree house and think of Ashley Maclean. She was making new memories. Deliberately she opened the book she'd brought with her. She was almost finished with it, and after a while the silence and the coolness lulled her and she became engrossed in her story.

"Hi!" A happy, child's voice nearly frightened Kate to death, and she looked down at a shining mass of golden hair and into a pair of familiar clear blue eyes.

CHAPTER THREE

Kate felt the blood drain from her face. In that split second she was back eighteen years, a shy and uncertain, very lonely ten-year-old.

She blinked, brought the present back into focus, and the world righted itself as she realized this child wasn't, couldn't be Ashley Maclean.

The golden hair, plaited the way Ashley sometimes plaited hers, was the same rich color, and so were the vivid blue eyes. But the shape of the mouth, the curve of the chin, were quite different. Yet there could be no mistaking the fact that this had to be Ashley's daughter, Kate acknowledged, realizing she had to have known this as soon as she saw the child.

By this time the young girl had climbed up onto the platform beside Kate, and she sat down easily on the old wooden packing crate, just the way Ashley used to do.

"You must be Kate, Kate Ballantyne," she said with a smile.

Kate opened her mouth, but no words came. She was fascinated by the way the child's eyes crinkled at the corners exactly the way her mother's did. Kate felt wild panic well up inside her, and she wanted to race back to her house, lock the door.

"My mother told me all about you," continued the child, oblivious to Kate's inner chaos.

"She" — Kate swallowed, trying to clear her throat — "she did?"

The child nodded, her grin widening. "She told me about all the adventures you had and the exciting things you did, and about all the scrapes you got into."

All? Kate swallowed again. No, Ashley wouldn't have told her daughter all of it. She felt a rush of distaste with herself at her thoughts and wiped a hand across her eyes. She had to pull herself together.

This was Ashley's daughter, Kate told herself. Part of Ashley. She surreptitiously studied the child. Yes, she was like Ashley but, Kate decided with a brief flare of antipathy, her mouth, her smile, was her father's.

But she was being unfair to the child, Kate berated herself. It was hardly the child's fault she resembled her father. And the child had nothing to do with any of this. She should know better, Kate told herself, for hadn't Kate herself suffered as a child by being part of the notorious Ballantynes?

"I'm Jennifer Andrews." The child held out a capable hand, and Kate automatically took it, the warmth of it engulfing her, clutching at her heart.

"My mother was your best friend. I knew you straightaway because Mum showed me your photo," Jennifer continued innocently.

"She did?" Kate repeated, her eyebrows rising in surprise, while deep inside her a tiny spark of pleasure flickered because Ashley had kept a photo of Kate. Was it the one they'd had taken at Ashley's sister's wedding, the photo they'd put in matching frames? Kate had hers, of herself and Ashley, in the bottom drawer of her dressing table. She rarely allowed herself to look at it, but she knew it was there. She often just touched the wooden frame.

"Yes. And you haven't changed hardly at all."

Kate smiled faintly at that. She felt as though she'd lived an entire lifetime since that time. "How long have you been here?" she asked unevenly. "I mean, when did you arrive in the Towers?"

"Yesterday. We were going to come up on Monday, but Mum had to do a few things." A quick frown came and went on the child's face. "We flew. It was really excellent. I hadn't been on an airplane since we were here last time."

"When was that?" Kate couldn't prevent herself from asking. Had Ashley been here before and Kate not known?

"When I was six. That's four years ago. We were

going to stay, but my father came and took us home."
Jennifer bit her lip.

The light seemed to have gone from the little girl's
eyes, and Kate wondered what caused the
unhappiness. It was obvious that something was wrong
and that it had something to do with her father.

"Did you know my father as well as Mum?" she
asked and Kate nodded.

"Yes, slightly," she replied carefully. "We met years
ago, before you were born."

Jennifer nodded. "Dad was working at the hospital
here. That's how he met Mum. He's a doctor you
know."

"Yes, I know." Kate searched around for something
to add to a conversation that had suddenly become
quietly serious. "He used to play football with your
uncles," she said to fill the silence that seemed to
hover over them.

"He doesn't play football any more. He works all
the time."

Kate nodded. "Doctors do work hard, don't they?"

Jennifer rested her elbow on her knee, her chin on
her hand, and a wave of pain clutched at Kate. Ashley
used to sit exactly like that.

Silence fell between them again, and Kate shifted
uneasily in her chair. The canvas creaked, and
Jennifer turned to look at her.

"My father replaces people's hearts. He's a really
important doctor," she said earnestly.

Kate wondered why she was surprised. The Dean
Andrews she had known had been a young intern.
He'd been handsome in a dark and intense sort of
way, but Kate had always thought he was self-centered

and petulant. And she'd burned with jealousy when Ashley had told her Dean had asked her to the movies. "I suppose that's why he has to work long hours."

"I guess."

"Do you have any brothers and sisters?" Kate asked to change the subject. Even now she found she couldn't talk easily about Ashley's husband.

"No, there's just me. Dad wanted more children but Mum couldn't have any more after me."

Kate glanced at the child in surprise. What had happened to Ashley?

"There were complications," Jennifer explained importantly. "Mum and I both nearly died."

"Oh." Kate swallowed, torturing herself with the thought of Ashley dying and no one telling her. Her heart contracted painfully at the thought. She didn't think she could take any more revelations this afternoon. "Did you tell your parents you were coming over here?"

Jennifer shook her head. "Not exactly. There's only Gran and me at home, and Gran's having a rest. But I'm sure Mum wouldn't mind. She's told me so much about the tree house I had to see it for myself." She looked around and sighed. "It's just like I imagined it would be. Can I come here sometimes?"

"Well," Kate hesitated. "I think you should ask your parents if you can first."

"It's just that my cousins are arriving today." Jennifer screwed up her nose. "And I might need to get away from them occasionally."

"Don't you like your cousins?"

Jennifer shrugged. "I don't really know them very

well. I haven't seen them for ages. When Aunt Belinda and Uncle Patrick came down to Melbourne last year they left the boys at home."

Belinda Maclean, Ashley's older sister, had married young, and her husband had been tragically killed before her first son was born. She'd returned to live with her parents, and Kate and Ashley had often babysat young Adam. A few years later Belinda married Patrick Harrison and went to live on his cane farm near Tully.

Kate couldn't recall much about the actual wedding, but she vividly remembered what happened afterward. She made herself push those particular memories out of her mind. "The boys?" she queried, and Jennifer pulled a face.

"Aunt Belinda has three sons. Can you believe that? Adam's fifteen, Mark's about twelve, and Josh is a bit older than me. What I want to know is, am I supposed to talk to them all day?" Jennifer held out her hands, palms upward. "I mean, what if I don't like them?"

Kate smiled. "What if you do?"

Jennifer giggled. "Mostly I don't like boys. They're always teasing you and stuff. Do you like boys?"

Kate felt herself flush. What did she reply to that? "Some are nice and some aren't, just like some girls are nice and some aren't."

"I guess." Jennifer stood up, pulling at a branch and peering through the leafy shield toward her grandparents' house. "Oh, no. There's the car. Mum's back from picking up Aunt Belinda and the boys. Uncle Pat's coming later. I didn't go with Mum because I couldn't fit in Gran's car with all of them and their luggage. And besides, I didn't want to be squashed in with all those boys." She wrinkled her small nose. "I guess I better go."

She climbed off the platform and onto the branch below. "Maybe you could come over and see us later?"

"Oh, I don't think . . . I, I'm going out," Kate finished lamely.

"Are you? Well, Mum will probably come over to call on you soon. Maybe tomorrow. She's looking forward to seeing you again."

With that the child disappeared, and Kate sat staring at the place where she'd been.

Ashley was looking forward to seeing her.

Kate stood up and felt her heart shift in her chest. What would she do if Ashley did come over? How would they react to seeing each other again? Would Ashley pretend there had been nothing between them? Dear God! Kate knew she wouldn't be able to bear it.

Then Kate heard voices, car doors slamming, and she found herself trying to look through the leafy branches as Jennifer had done. The branches all but obscured the house now, so she pulled at a thinner branch, holding it back so she could get a better view.

A group of people were walking along the side of the Maclean house heading for the back door where Jennifer stood waiting for them. No one would guess she had just slid between the loose palings of the back fence.

Kate picked out Belinda. She looked a little older, but Kate recognized her. She would be thirty-four now. Beside her carrying a couple of suitcases was a gangling teenager who had to be Adam. The second boy was a redhead like his father, and the youngest had Belinda's dark hair.

As they rounded the corner of the house, Kate saw the figure they had been partially concealing. Kate recognized her immediately too. She walked with an easy grace that struck a nerve deep inside Kate. Her golden hair was much shorter now, but it glistened in the sunlight just as it always had. She raised one hand to brush the front back from her face in a gesture that was so familiar to Kate she heard herself moan softly.

"Oh, Ashley," someone said thickly, and then Kate realized it was herself.

At that moment Ashley turned her head, looked toward the back fence and the top of the huge tree, and Kate drew back in alarm, letting go of the branch. Would Ashley have seen the movement, caught her spying on them?

Kate stepped across and quickly lowered herself onto the branch, fumbled for hand- and footholds, stumbled down the ladder, and ran back to the house. By the time she reached her bedroom she was breathless. She sank down on the side of the bed and tried to calm herself.

Before she could prevent herself she had opened her dressing-table drawer and lifted out the photograph. It was a head-and-shoulders study, and Ashley smiled back at her, beside her own far more serious face. Kate turned and sat down on the bed again.

The photo had been taken at Belinda's wedding by the official photographer. Ashley had made him take one of her with Kate, organizing them both to stand close together, arm in arm. Kate didn't think it was such a great shot of herself, but at least it was a photo of her and Ashley together.

"Oh, Ashley," she said again and lay back against her pillows.

Belinda's wedding, well, afterward, had been the beginning.

Ashley had walked Kate home after the reception, which had been held in a huge tent in the Maclean backyard. They were both still in their wedding finery, Ashley in her mauve chiffon bridesmaid's dress and Kate in a plain blue dress she'd bought for the occasion.

Kate's aunt was in the back room dozing in front of the television, and after they'd given her a short description of the wedding they'd gone into Kate's room.

"I hope the photo of us comes out. I'm going to get us matching frames so we can have them on our dressing tables," Ashley said as she kicked off her shoes and threw herself onto Kate's bed.

"It'll be okay of you, but I always look like a dork in photos." Kate moved Ashley's legs aside so she could sit beside her.

"You do not." She smiled up at Kate. "You look great. Intelligent. And beautiful."

Kate gave a disbelieving laugh. "Liar, liar, pants on fire."

Ashley laughed and then sobered. "I don't know why you always put yourself down. I think you're beautiful."

And when Kate was with Ashley was the only time Kate did feel beautiful.

"Sorry I didn't get over to see you last night." Ashley rolled her eyes. "I didn't finish practice until late, and then Mum had us all running around in

44

circles making sure everything was just right for Belinda's big day."

"I guess there was a lot to organize."

"After going through all this the past few weeks I think I'll elope." She looked up at Kate. "If I ever get married, that is."

Something twisted inside Kate, and she looked away. "You will," she said as evenly as she could.

"I don't think I want to," Ashley declared with feeling.

"Why not?" Kate asked, secretly pleased by that statement.

Ashley shrugged. "T. J. tried to kiss me," she said without preamble, and Kate gave her a startled look.

"When?"

"Behind the stands at softball practice yesterday afternoon."

"We aren't supposed to go behind the stands," Kate began, and Ashley gave her an old-fashioned look.

"Everybody goes behind the stands, Kate," she said dryly.

Kate had never been behind the stands but she let that pass. "Did you — what did you do? When he kissed you?"

"Pushed him over the fence."

Kate bit off a laugh, and Ashley giggled.

"Well, he deserved it. I don't want anyone kissing me unless I want to be kissed. I mean, kissing is pretty personal, don't you think, Kate?"

Kate flushed. She had never envisaged kissing a boy, couldn't even begin to imagine it, let alone anything else. In fact Kate wouldn't let herself think about Belinda and her new husband and what they'd be doing tonight, although Ashley's brothers had teased the happy couple unmercifully with nudges and innuendos.

"Apart from that," Ashley continued, "T. J. was really sloppy." She wiped her mouth. "Yuck! I felt like he was trying to swallow me whole."

Kate shuddered and wrinkled her nose. "It makes me feel sick."

"What? T. J. or kissing?"

"Kissing."

"We'll be expected to, you know."

"We don't have to if we don't want to. You just said so."

"No, I mean if you fall in love."

Kate frowned. "We're only fifteen. That's too young to fall in love." She felt a moment of confusion, and suddenly disquieted, she pushed the feeling away.

Ashley laughed. "We're nearly sixteen, and lots of girls in our class have been kissing for years." She paused for emphasis. "Kissing and more, I might add."

"More?" Kate repeated, her mouth suddenly dry.

Ashley pulled a face. "You know."

Kate blushed. "You mean — They have? Who? How do you know?"

"They've told me, that's how I know." Ashley tsked. "Honestly, Kate. Sometimes I think you go around with your eyes closed."

Kate sighed. "I'm not like you, Ash. People tell you things. They don't tell me."

"I tell you things."

Kate smiled. "You tell me things all the time, even when I don't want to know."

"Don't you want to know about kissing?" Ashley teased.

"No, I don't think so."

"Well, I think you should know all about it. In fact, I think you should be practicing now so you'll be ready when you really want to kiss someone."

Kate grimaced. "I don't know anyone I'd want to kiss." That same uncomfortable feeling twisted in her stomach, and her gaze was drawn to Ashley's lips. Quickly Kate looked away. "Or anyone who'd want to kiss me," she added quickly.

"What about Tim?"

Kate was horrified. "Your brother?"

"I think he likes you."

"He's nearly nineteen," Kate said in absolute dismay.

"Mmm. I guess he is a bit old. But he does like you, I'm sure of it."

Kate didn't think she'd ever be able to look Tim Maclean in the face again.

"Well, what about Mike Dunstan?" Ashley began reeling off names and Kate shook her head emphatically.

"No way." She looked at Ashley. "Do you want to kiss anyone?"

Ashley gave the question some consideration. "No. Not really. I guess not." She looked at Kate and chewed her bottom lip. "We could practice on each other."

Every nerve in Kate's body tensed. "What" — she swallowed — "what do you mean?"

"Well, we could, you know, try it out on each other. We could work out the best way to do it, and then we'd know how without having to kiss guys we didn't like."

"Oh." Kate was having trouble formulating words.

"I think it's a great idea," Ashley was saying, bouncing into a sitting position beside Kate. "Want to try?"

"You mean now?"

"Why not?"

Kate looked around. "Well . . ."

"No one can see us and your aunt's probably well asleep in front of the telly by now. Besides, we'd hear her coming down the hallway if she did wake up."

Kate swallowed.

"It's perfect. Wouldn't you rather kiss me than any of the boys in our class?"

Kate was hot all over. A million thoughts and sensations skittered about inside her.

"Okay?" Ashley persevered, but still Kate hesitated. And then Ashley sat up, leaned across, put her hand on Kate's shoulder, and her lips touched Kate's.

They felt soft and sweet, and Kate's heart beat madly in her chest.

Ashley drew back, and Kate had to stop herself from following her, desperately not wanting the kiss to end.

"Okay?" Ashley said again, softly this time, and Kate nodded.

And then Ashley kissed her again. This time her soft lips opened a little and her tongue tip traced the outline of Kate's mouth. Kate moaned softly, her stomach turning to water. She moved closer, her young breasts tingling where they touched Ashley's. And suddenly their arms were around each other. Ashley's tongue was inside Kate's mouth, and Kate was beyond reason, way beyond rationality.

When Ashley pulled away, they were both breathless. Their eyes met and held, and Kate was sure the earth rocked crazily on its axis.

"That was —" Ashley began and swallowed. "That wasn't anything like kissing T. J.," she said unevenly.

Kate's heart sank. Hadn't Ashley liked it? Did that mean she didn't want to repeat it? Kate wanted to go on kissing Ashley forever.

"Can we do that again?" Ashley asked softly, and eagerly Kate leaned forward.

This time she kissed Ashley, moved into her arms, and held her close. It was a long time before they sat apart.

Ashley picked up Kate's hand, held it lightly in hers. "You know, I've wanted to do that for the longest time."

"You have? Well, why didn't you? Before, I mean."

"I thought you might think it was, you know, gross or something."

"No. It was wonderful."

And it had been wonderful. Kate could still burn from the memory of that kiss. She gazed at Ashley's face in the photograph, and a tear ran down her cheek.

"Oh, Ashley," she murmured and turned her face into the pillow.

Kate spent a restless night and woke up tired and heavy eyed. Her first thoughts were of Ashley. She lay in bed and sighed and then sat bolt upright. What if Ashley came over to visit her as Jennifer had said she intended to do? It was Sunday, and Ashley would know that Kate wasn't at work.

In a fit of agitation Kate pulled on a pair of shorts and a loose T-shirt and climbed into her car. In no time at all she was on the road out of town and heading toward the Burdekin River.

If she'd accepted Rosemary's invitation to go with her this weekend, none of this would have happened. She wouldn't have met Ashley's daughter, and she wouldn't have seen Ashley. And she wouldn't have dreamed those disturbingly unsatisfying dreams about her.

With resolution Kate tightened her grip on the steering wheel and increased her speed. She would pick a spot on the riverbank and relax.

Kate drove back into the Towers late in the afternoon, and although she was physically tired she felt more in command of herself. She'd driven out to the bridge, parked with all the picnickers, and sat beneath a shady tree to eat the fruit she'd brought with her. The air was heavy with heat and the sounds of people enjoying the Sunday afternoon.

After lunch she'd stayed under her tree watching a family play an energetic game of cricket. Eventually she'd picked up and finished the book she was reading, and then she'd opened the Leigh Mossman book, *Gold Fever*.

She read the first chapter and could see why the book had become a best-seller. Kate had to acknowledge that it certainly held her interest. In fact, she had been sorry she had to put the book down to drive home. She decided she'd continue reading it after dinner.

With a much more calm and positive feeling she turned into the driveway of home only to brake suddenly as she saw the figure sitting on her front steps. With the engine idling, Kate could only stare as the woman stood up, the setting sun burnishing her short golden hair.

CHAPTER FOUR

Ashley walked down the worn, wooden stairs and across the short distance to the car. "Hello, Kate," she said with a tentative smile.

Her eyes were narrowed against the glare from the setting sun, so Kate couldn't read the expression in them. She simply sat there and looked at Ashley, her gaze drawn to the strained, hesitant smile on Ashley's lips.

Kate swallowed and found her voice. "I, I'll just

put the car away." With a crunch of gears she steered the car into the carport.

Taking a deep breath she picked up her bag and climbed out of the car, carefully shutting the door behind her. To Kate, every action she took seemed delayed, a half beat behind her thought processes. She paused to gather her composure before walking back to where Ashley stood waiting for her.

"Have you been here long?" she asked Ashley stiltedly, cringing inwardly at her inanity. "I mean, have you been waiting long?"

A flicker of an indiscernible emotion crossed Ashley's face. "Waiting long? Ages," she said, looking directly into Kate's eyes, and then she smiled crookedly. "No, not long really. I'd just decided you'd gone out to dinner, and I was about to go home."

"Oh." Kate shifted her bag from one hand to the other, realizing her palms were damp.

Her glance went to Ashley and quickly away again in case Ashley saw her looking. She didn't dare allow herself the luxury of letting her eyes linger on Ashley's familiar face, her so familiar body. If she did she might lose what little composure she had.

Although how she would react if she did relinquish her self-control she couldn't imagine. Kate liked to think she'd coolly demand of Ashley why she thought she could simply turn up and Kate would accept her return without rancor.

Kate could almost laugh at herself. Cool and composed? She was far from that, and she suspected she hadn't the savoir faire to carry it off.

Yet her fleeting glance seemed to take in every

inch of Ashley's attractiveness. If she closed her eyes, Kate knew she would be able to see Ashley in minute detail.

Physically, Ashley was about five-four, three or four inches shorter than Kate, and where Kate was lean to the point of androgyny, Ashley's body was well defined and so obviously feminine. Her eyes were still that clear, arresting blue, and the light freckles Kate loved still dusted the bridge of her nose. Her hair, worn short now, sat back over the sides of her head, the front falling naturally across her forehead.

Ashley wore a pair of tailored navy-blue shorts and a plain white T-shirt that accentuated the rounded swell of her breasts, the curve of her hips. Ashley looked cool and fresh, and Kate, in her own far-from-new shorts and shirt, crumpled from her day at the river, felt gauche and unsophisticated.

"Can I come in?" Ashley motioned toward the house, and Kate hesitated.

All her instincts shrieked inside her demanding that she refuse, that she not allow this woman, this so achingly familiar, so beautiful woman, anywhere near her. But deep inside her a small voice rose above the screaming misgivings.

"Sure," Kate heard herself say, and she turned on rubbery legs to lead the way up the steps.

As she fumbled with the key, Kate's mind played over the sight of the other woman. Of Ashley now. She hadn't changed that much really. Her figure had always been curved in the right places, her hips rounded, her waist narrow. And Kate could still remember the delight she'd always felt as she ran her lips over Ashley's full breasts.

An arrow of desire spiraled downward to blossom

between her legs and Kate's mouth went dry. And she was only partially reassured by the knowledge that Ashley couldn't see her face.

Hurriedly Kate stepped through the lattice gateway and across the wide veranda to unlock the solid front door. She led the way into the living room and turned as Ashley stepped inside.

"Would you like some coffee? Tea?" Kate asked politely, but Ashley shook her head.

She pushed her hair back from her forehead in a gesture that Kate remembered so well. Ashley always did that when she was nervous or ill at ease. Well, Kate could understand how Ashley felt. She was more than a little discomfited herself. Her insides felt like butterflies were square dancing in there.

Did Ashley remember the last time they'd seen each other? That awful scene seemed to Kate to sit heavily between them as they stood in the living room, the width of the carpet square separating them.

And suddenly Kate was back those ten long years, and they were together in Ashley's bedroom in the large sprawling house on the other side of the back fence.

The room was small and painted pale pink, and the single bed still had the lace canopy that Ashley thought was kids' stuff but couldn't bring herself to remove. Kate and Ashley had spent hours together in that room as they grew up, playing, talking, doing homework. And since that electrifying moment after Belinda's wedding, when they'd occasionally had the house to themselves, they'd spent the time in Ashley's narrow bed making love. Of course, they'd had to be careful and they always were.

* * * * *

That day Ashley's father and brothers were still at work, and Ashley's mother and Kate's aunt were at a meeting that always kept them until late.

Kate sighed and ran her fingertip over Ashley's breasts, feeling the film of perspiration that still coated Ashley's skin in the aftermath of their love-making.

"That was fantastic. Do you realize it's been a whole week since we've been able to get together? I've wanted to kiss every inch of you so much I thought I'd die in history lesson this afternoon." Kate lowered her lips to gently tease Ashley's nipple, and Ashley murmured deep in her throat.

"Would have been better than whatever invasion we were supposed to be reading about, don't you think?" Ashley laughed. "Wish we had time to start all over again." She moved impossibly closer to Kate.

Their bodies were molded in familiar togetherness, and they kissed lingeringly.

"I love you," Ashley said softly.

Kate nibbled her way along Ashley's chin and snuggled into the curve of Ashley's neck. "Kate?"

"Mmm." Kate closed her eyes and drew in the intoxicating scent of Ashley's hair.

"Kate? We should talk about —" She paused. "I want to talk about Dean and the football club dance," Ashley began, and Kate lifted her head to look at her.

"That was ages ago. I'm sorry I was so, well, angry about it all. I admit I was really upset when you went with him, and I had the very worst time watching you together, but I think I understand why you did. I mean, I guess we do have to pretend we, well, you

know. Anyway, you haven't been out with him since."
She looked across at the frown on Ashley's face.
"Have you?"

"No." Ashley said slowly. "No, of course not. Not
since the dance. I ... I would have told you."

When Ashley told Kate she was attending the
football club dance with Dean, they had had a
dreadful argument that had continued at the dance. It
had ended in Ashley turning on her heel and
marching off, leaving Kate hurt and confused.

They'd avoided each other at school for the next
week, and Kate had spent a miserable Saturday night
alone, imagining Dean Andrews dancing with Ashley,
holding her close to his broad chest, a gleam of
triumph in his eyes.

And then late on Sunday afternoon Ashley had
telephoned Kate to say she was alone and could she
see Kate. Kate had rushed over, and a pale and tired
Ashley had been waiting for her. Ashley had clutched
Kate fiercely to her, sobbing an apology into Kate's
neck.

They'd ended up in Ashley's bedroom, holding each
other close. It seemed to Kate that Ashley couldn't
bear to let her go, and that had been fine with Kate.
When Kate had begun caressing her, Ashley had
stopped her, telling Kate she just wanted to be held.
That was also fine with Kate. She'd simply held
Ashley in her arms, breathing in her sweetness.

Now, weeks later, this was the first time Ashley
had spoken of Dean Andrews.

"Well, if you haven't been out with him, that's all
right then," Kate said with mock seriousness. "And I
haven't been out with Phillip either." Kate groaned.
"The last time I went with him to the movies it was

awful. When he tried to kiss me good night and stuck his tongue in my mouth, I was almost sick."

"Kate, there's something I want to talk to you about." The tone in Ashley's voice made Kate still. "I can't talk about it to Mum, and I'm scared."

"Scared? Ash, what about? If you're worried about anyone finding out about us —"

"No, it's not that. God, I wish it was." Ashley ran a hand over her eyes. "I'm scared you'll hate me when I tell you."

"I could never hate you, Ashley," Kate said sincerely. "I love you. You know that."

"Oh, Kate." Ashley clasped Kate to her. "Let's run away together. Now."

Kate laughed softly. "Wish we could. But it's only another couple of months. After Christmas we'll be able to go down to Brisbane to university. We can share a flat and be together all the time like we planned."

"Kate, what if —" Ashley stopped and bit her lip.

"What if what? What if we don't get scholarships to uni? We will. But if not we'll just go down south and get jobs. We'll be fine. You'll see."

Ashley was holding Kate so tightly she had to ease some space between them to take a breath.

"I need air, Ash." Kate made a show of deep breathing. "So, does this mean you love me to death?" she asked lightly.

Ashley sighed. "I love you more than you know."

"And I love you, too," Kate said and kissed Ashley's soft, eager mouth before ruefully drawing back. "I guess we should be getting dressed. What's the time?"

Ashley glanced over Kate's head at her bedside clock. "We've got a little longer."

"Great," Kate murmured appreciatively. "You feel divine." She ran her hand down the indentation of Ashley's spine and over the curve of her buttocks and pulled Ashley against her again.

Ashley's leg slipped between hers, and a spark of desire burst into flame in Kate's center. She arched her body against Ashley's, her lips finding Ashley's, and they kissed with renewed passion.

"What — ? Oh, my God!"

Neither of them had heard the footsteps in the carpeted hallway or heard Ashley's mother open the bedroom door. They both turned, startled, to look toward the voice.

Patsy Maclean clung to the doorknob with one hand, while the other hand clutched at her throat in horror. "Oh, my God!" she repeated. "What are — ? What — ?"

Kate's muscles had turned to jelly, and she was unable to move. She continued to hold Ashley to her as they both stared at the older woman.

Ashley was the first to rouse. She grabbed at the bedsheet, pulling it over their naked bodies.

"Mum, I can explain," she began, and her mother drew a rasping breath.

"Get dressed, both of you, and then come into the kitchen." She closed the door with a subdued click that seemed to explode into the small space.

Kate turned back to Ashley. "What can we do?" she whispered, feeling hysteria rise inside her.

"I don't know," Ashley said thickly. "I don't — Oh, God, Kate! What *can* we do?"

Kate fought to calm her still pounding heart. She drew a deep breath. "We'll have to tell the truth, I guess. That we love each other. What else can we do?"

"Mum won't understand. No one will," Ashley cried. "What if she tells Dad? And your aunt?"

Kate's mouth went dry. This couldn't be happening.

Then Ashley seemed to pull herself together. "We'd better get dressed," she said flatly and pushed Kate toward the edge of the bed.

Kate sat up and shakily swung her legs to the floor. She stumbled as she reached for her clothes and Ashley grasped her arm, steadying her.

"They'll have to understand, Kate. Won't they?" she asked desperately as they reached for their clothes.

Ashley was all fingers as she struggled to fasten her bra. Kate stopped to help her, turning Ashley back to face her.

"Oh, Kate. What a mess." Ashley's voice caught on a sob.

"Shh." Kate kissed her tenderly. "Just remember that whatever happens, I love you," she said earnestly. Ashley nodded.

They finished dressing, and Kate took Ashley's hand and squeezed it before they left the room and walked the short distance to the kitchen.

Patsy Maclean didn't look at them when they entered the room. She had made herself a cup of tea and sat at the table, the floral china cup clutched in both hands. Kate could see she was shaking, could hear the rattle of the cup in the saucer.

Kate started to speak, but Ashley put a gentle hand on her arm.

"Mum, look, this isn't what you think," she began, and her mother turned a strained face to look at her.

"It isn't? Then I don't know what it is."

Kate glanced at Ashley, at the drawn paleness of her face, and she straightened her backbone, lifting her chin. "Mrs. Maclean, we . . . Ashley and I . . . we love each other," she said levelly.

Patsy Maclean angrily stood up, spilling her tea, her chair tipping over backward. Kate felt Ashley jump beside her at the noise, and Kate had to make herself hold her ground when she wanted to run.

"Love?" Ashley's mother bit out. "You don't know what you're talking about. That's not love. Not normal love. No daughter of mine is —" She shook her head. "I can't even say that word." She turned to Ashley, and Ashley seemed to shrink. "How could you do this, Ashley?"

"Mrs. Maclean —" Kate began again, and Patsy turned on her with a glare of dislike.

"Don't talk to me, Kate Ballantyne. I knew I shouldn't have let you get so friendly with my daughter. I knew there was bad blood in your family. Everyone knows about the Ballantynes, their lying, thieving ways. I should have gone with my better judgment, but I felt sorry for you, orphaned, alone in that cold house with Jane Ballantyne. But no. I welcomed you into my home, treated you just like my own daughter, and this is how you choose to repay me."

"Mum, please," Ashley pleaded. "We didn't *choose* to fall in love. It just happened."

"In love!" Patsy almost spat. "Stop saying that." She folded her arms and paced across the kitchen and back again. "You don't fall in love with a girl. You find a nice young man like I did, like your sister did. Well, I know what's to be done." Patsy took a steadying breath and turned, picking up the chair. "If you can't find a nice boy then one will be found for you. Both of you."

"I don't want a nice boy, Mum," Ashley said quietly. "And neither does Kate."

"I don't want to discuss this any more, Ashley. I have to start dinner. And Kate, I think it would be best if you went home. I'll be talking to your aunt."

Kate stood fixed to the spot, not knowing what to do.

"And that Phillip Walker, the one who's always hanging around you," Patsy continued. "It's time you encouraged his interest."

"I'm not . . . I don't like Phillip Walker," Kate said softly.

"I don't think that matters right now." Patsy Maclean took the dishcloth and mopped up her spilled tea.

"Mrs. Maclean," Kate began, her vocal cords stiff. "I know all this has been, is, something of a shock to you, but I'd prefer it if you didn't speak to my aunt. I should do that myself."

Ashley's mother gave her a withering look. "I don't think what you prefer should be taken into consideration. What I do know is the fact that Ashley is my responsibility. You're Jane Ballantyne's, and she'll have to deal with you in her own way. But one thing's for sure, you two won't be seeing each other for some time."

"Mum, please," Ashley appealed.

"That's enough, Ashley," her mother snapped. "I don't want to hear any more about it."

"It won't change the way Ashley and I feel about each other," Kate put in quietly, and Patsy's mouth thinned.

"The two of you have been too close for too long. Now it's time to spend some time with young men."

"We don't like young men," Ashley snapped, and her mother shook her head, gazing at her daughter as though she hadn't really seen her before.

"I can't understand this, Ashley," she said in despair. "You've never — you said you enjoyed your dates with Dean Andrews."

Kate was looking at Ashley and saw the flash of desperation that crossed Ashley's face.

"Oh, Mum. I told you what I knew you wanted to hear. I —"

To Kate's consternation, Ashley began to cry. Kate wanted to put her arms around her, but Patsy's look prevented her.

"You don't understand, Mum. Oh, God! This is such a mess," Ashley finished in despair.

"A mess of your own making. How could you do this to your father and me? It's" — she shook her head — "it's not normal."

"Normal?" Ashley repeated angrily. "And is it normal prostituting yourself having sex with a man even when you don't want to?"

"Ash," Kate murmured, but Ashley's gaze was fixed on her mother.

"You don't know what you're talking about, Ashley," Patsy Maclean said dismissively.

"Don't I? I've tried a man, Mother, and believe me, I prefer women."

Kate's startled eyes met Ashley's, and the other girl looked quickly away.

"Please try to understand, Mum. I love Kate."

"Stop saying that."

"You know, I think you'd be less upset if I told you I was pregnant," Ashley angrily cried at her mother. "Well, would you? Would you be less angry with me if I said I was pregnant?"

Patsy Maclean ran a hand over her eyes. "Ashley, go to your room. I just can't take any more of this tonight. Kate, I think you should leave."

Kate stood undecided, and then Ashley sighed, her tense body suddenly slumping. She turned to Kate. "You'd better go, Kate." She reached out her hand, rubbed it softly on Kate's bare arm. "I'll talk to you later."

Their eyes met, held, and then Kate nodded. She turned and left the house to walk slowly home.

Ashley had phoned her a few days later, making vague promises about moving to Brisbane. And then had come the phone call from Ashley that had broken Kate's young heart. Ashley had told Kate she was going to marry Dean Andrews and would Kate come to the wedding. Kate had vehemently refused, and with hindsight she'd realized from Ashley's tone that the invitation to her wedding had been a token one.

A week later Kate knew she had to try to talk to Ashley one more time, but Ashley's mother had answered the phone. Patsy Maclean had verified that the wedding would take place the next week and that Patsy would appreciate it if Kate would keep away and not put Ashley under any more strain than she was already under.

At the time Kate had thought Ashley's defiant statement to her mother that she had slept with a man had been pure bravado, but when the rumors of

Ashley's pregnancy had begun circulating at her hurried marriage, Kate had begun to wonder about that and Ashley's integrity. All she knew was Ashley's damning silence.

And now Ashley was here, and Kate hadn't seen her in ten years.

"You've painted the house." Ashley's voice dragged Kate back into the present. "It looks great."

"Thank you. Aunt Jane always talked about repainting it, but she never got around to having it done."

"I like the softer, lighter colors," Ashley said. "It makes the rooms look bigger."

They stood in a strained silence, and Kate's nerve endings screamed as a mixture of wanting and wrath clutched in the pit of her stomach. How could Ashley stand there making idle conversation after what she'd done? How could she have the barefaced nerve?

"Perhaps a cup of tea would be nice."

Kate blinked, trying to compute the words. "Tea?" Kate swallowed. "All right." She dropped her bag onto the chair and walked back into the hallway, her muscles taut as she felt Ashley following her into the kitchen. "Unless you'd like a tamarind drink."

"You have some?" Ashley asked in amazement. "That would be great. I haven't had that since . . . She paused. "For so long."

Since you left, Kate wanted to finish for her, but she simply nodded and took the tall jug of iced tea-like liquid from the refrigerator. She poured two tall glasses and added a liberal amount of ice.

When she turned she found Ashley watching her. Disconcerted, Kate handed her a glass, being extra careful not to allow their hands to touch.

"Mmm," Ashley murmured as she held the glass up. "Even the smell of it takes me back." She took a taste. "Wonderful. Remember how great it was sitting in the shady tree house on a hot day, drinking this?"

Remember? Kate wanted to shout at her. *Don't talk about remembering. You have no right after what you did.* "Yes," she said flatly, and Ashley glanced at her quickly.

Kate drew herself together. "Shall we go back into the living room?"

"Okay." Ashley turned, and this time Kate followed her along the hallway.

And Kate found herself watching the back of Ashley's head, the way the tendrils of her short hair fanned the back of her neck, her straight back beneath her white shirt, the way her hips moved as she walked, her shapely legs. And Kate yearned to reach out, stop her, draw her warm soft body back against hers, slip her arms around Ashley's waist, let her hands move upward to clasp her full breasts.

Then they were back in the living room, and Kate shakily motioned for Ashley to sit down on the couch. Kate turned to move her bag so she could sit opposite Ashley on the single chair. As she picked up her bag, the paperback copy of *Gold Fever* fell onto the floor. Kate bent over to retrieve it and shove it back in her bag.

As she sat down she saw Ashley looking at the book. "It's set in the Towers. Have you read it?" Kate asked.

Soft color washed Ashley's face. "Yes, I have. What did you think of it?"

"I only started it this afternoon actually. But it's really good so far. I didn't want to put it down."

"What part are you up to?"

"The heroine, Clare, has just arrived in the Towers after finding out she has family here." This was an innocuous subject, and Kate clutched at the normality of it. "The book's been really well researched. The journey up from Brisbane is authentic, and the description of the township at the height of the gold rush is colorful. I could almost feel I was there in the main street as it teemed with rough miners lighting their cigars with ten-pound notes."

Kate stopped and looked across at Ashley. The ten years between might never have been. Here they sat discussing books the way they used to do. Kate's mouth went dry, and she swallowed.

"Do you still prefer reading mysteries?" Ashley asked softly, and it seemed to Kate that Ashley might be feeling the same nostalgia Kate was.

Kate nodded. "Mostly."

A heavy silence fell, and Kate could hear the ponderous ticking of her aunt's old mantel clock.

Ashley's chair creaked as she stood up. Kate tensed, but Ashley was only walking over to the sideboard, her back to Kate as she bent over to look at the photographs there: The sepia shades of her grandmother and grandfather Ballantyne in their dark, high-necked clothing so impractical for the hot, tropical north Queensland climate. Kate's parents' wedding photo. A head-and-shoulders shot of her Aunt Jane as a young woman, austere even then. And one of an uncertain Kate, an unsmiling ten-year-old taken not long before she arrived to live with Jane Ballantyne.

"I was sorry to hear about your aunt's death. Mum forgot to tell me when it happened." Ashley turned back to look at Kate. "I was going to write but, by then, well..." The end of the sentence hung between them.

"She fell and broke her hip," Kate said quickly to fill the incendiary void. "She never fully recovered from it, although she did come home from hospital. She grew more frail and just faded away."

"Did you — ?" Ashley looked down at her drink. "When did you come back to the Towers?"

"When Aunt Jane had her accident. She needed someone here with her. So I came home."

"And got a job in the local library?"

Kate nodded. "Just before Aunt Jane died. I was working for the Brisbane City Council Library Service before that."

Ashley smiled faintly. "I'm not surprised you went into library work. You always loved books."

"So did you." The words were out before Kate could take them back. She'd vowed not to let the conversation slide below a superficial level. "What did you do?"

"Do?" Ashley grimaced into her drink, absently swirling the ice in the bottom. "Nothing. I have absolutely no useful qualifications," she said bitterly.

Kate looked at her, at the play of emotions that crossed her face, and something shifted in the region of her heart. In those short seconds she knew Ashley was not happy.

Ashley glanced up and her gaze held Kate's. "A

waste, wasn't it?" she said wryly. "I became a dutiful wife and mother. In that order. Always in that order. And I wasn't very good at either."

Kate didn't know what to say. "I met Jennifer yesterday."

"She told me."

"She . . . she seems a great kid."

Ashley's face softened. "She is that, even if I do say so myself. Jen's all I've got to show for the last ten years."

"She looks very much like you." The words had to fight their way around a knot of pain that had lodged itself in Kate's throat.

"Mum thinks so, too." Ashley grimaced. "But Dean wanted a son to carry on the good name, so I failed again. And then, no more children."

"Jennifer told me." Kate stopped, embarrassed that Ashley would now know she had been discussing Ashley with her daughter.

"You two seem to have had a pretty in-depth conversation."

"Not really. We just . . ." Kate sought the right words.

"It's all right, Kate. I know what my daughter's like. She's wonderfully open and remarkably well-adjusted, considering." Ashley made a negating movement of her head. "I sometimes wonder how that happened, how two absolutely dysfunctional people like Dean and me, managed that. But anyway," she continued, "suffice to say Jen saved my sanity."

She pushed herself away from where she was leaning her elbow on the sideboard. "But enough of that. Tell me about you."

Kate shrugged. "Nothing much to tell."

"Are you" — she paused for an almost imperceptible moment — "involved with anyone?"

Kate felt warm color wash her cheeks. Rosemary Greig's face appeared momentarily in her mind's eye, but she blinked it away. After all, they had made no commitment to each other.

Tell Ashley you're involved with Rosemary, self-preservation demanded. *Tell her you're happy and contented with your relationship. Tell Ashley you got over her and life went on . . .*

"Involved? Not exactly," she replied carefully, even as she told herself Ashley had no right to an answer.

"Not exactly?" Ashley repeated and raised one fine dark eyebrow. She walked over and sat down in the chair opposite Kate. "That's very ambiguous."

Kate held her gaze. "I've never married. I'm not engaged," she said evenly. "But I am seeing a friend, on a casual basis."

A heavy silence engulfed them again, and it was Ashley who broke it.

"Male or female?" she asked, and Kate's face flamed.

CHAPTER FIVE

They stood looking at each other as Kate sought to formulate a reply to the audacious question.

"Does it matter?" she asked levelly.

"To acquaintances, I guess not. But we used to be friends."

"Friends?" Kate bit off a sharp laugh. "Oh, yes. We used to be friends. *Used to be* is the operative phrase."

Ashley sighed. "I wish . . ." She shook her head. "Well, as your aunt used to say, *If wishes were horses, then beggars would ride.*"

Silence fell again, and Kate shifted in her chair.

"It's not Phillip Walker, is it?" Ashley's words had Kate glancing back at her in surprise.

"Phillip?"

"The friend you're seeing on a casual basis?" Ashley elaborated.

"No, of course not. Whatever gave you that idea?"

"Mum said she'd seen you and Phillip lunching together last week."

"I see." Kate wondered if her first thought that Patsy Maclean might have been warning her daughter off Kate was at all paranoid. "Phillip's my boss in a sense, and I've never had lunch with him. I don't know where your mother got the impression we were going out. Actually, Phillip's still in the middle of a divorce."

"Is he? There's a lot of it around," Ashley added wryly. "You never went out with Phillip Walker after . . ." There was that same imperceptible pause again. ". . . after I left?"

"No, I didn't. When I went to the University of Queensland in Brisbane, he went to James Cook University in Townsville. He married one of the Burtons from there."

Ashley's blue eyes held Kate's for long moments. "I'm glad it wasn't, isn't, Phillip," she said softly, and Kate's heartbeats leaped in excitement at the same ephemeral concept that Ashley might still care. And then she silently berated herself for her foolishness.

"Phillip was always such a nonentity," Ashley continued into the heavy tension that seemed to radiate from Kate. "I can't see that he'd have changed over the years. Is he still a crushing bore?"

Kate pulled herself together. Talking about Phillip

Walker forced any thoughts that Ashley still cared to the back of her mind. "Phillip a bore? Yes, I'm afraid he still is. Pernaps more so if that's possible. Phillip's great with numbers so he's a good town clerk but . . ." She shrugged wryly.

"Well, if it's not Phillip, who is it?" Ashley persisted.

"No one you know."

"Ah." Ashley continued to watch Kate. "So it's a best kept secret."

"Oh, for heaven's sake." Kate's nerves were so jumpy she had to move. She stood up and faced the other woman. "Is it that important? If you want to know if I'm a lesbian, then, yes, I am. Are you satisfied? I still prefer women. I always have."

"I'm glad," Ashley said softly, and Kate swallowed, sure Ashley would be able to hear her racing heartbeats.

"I don't know why," she said, suddenly tired of the emotion-charged conversation. "It made no difference ten years ago, so why should it be so all-important now? Unless you subscribe to the view that it's caused by a failure to develop emotionally past adolescence. Then I guess you'd say I needed a shrink."

"You'd be the last person I'd say needed to see a psychiatrist," Ashley said softly.

Kate sighed. "Some people may say that's debatable." She shifted from one foot to the other, trying to release some of the tension that held her tautly, and she wondered if she could take much more of this. Perhaps she should simply ask Ashley to leave.

Kate glanced pointedly at the clock. "Won't your mother, your husband be wondering where you are?"

"I told Mum I was going for a walk, which I did. Belinda took Jen and the boys out to the weir for the afternoon. And Dean, well, Dean's not here."

"When's he arriving?"

"He's not."

Kate examined this piece of information. Something in Ashley's tone made her feel suddenly hot, and she swallowed, trying to rein in her galloping imagination.

"Jennifer told me he was a busy heart surgeon."

"Oh, yes, he's busy. As a doctor Dean's rather brilliant." She pulled a face. "As a husband and father, well, he wasn't so great."

Past tense. Kate clutched at that, but for the life of her she could think of nothing to say.

"We'll be divorced as of the end of the month."

"Divorced?" Kate swallowed, suddenly numb. "I'm sorry," she added banally.

"Are you?" Ashley was looking into the almost melted ice in her glass. "I'm not. These ten years have been pure hell."

Kate's mouth went dry. "I'm —" She stopped. What could she say?

"Surprised?" Ashley's dark brows rose inquiringly. "You can't be. You warned me that Dean and I scarcely knew each other when I told you we were getting married."

Kate felt the familiar pain of that rejection, and anger rose inside her. "Your mother told me it was none of my business. And perhaps she was right. I mean, I didn't really know enough about you and Dean to comment on that, Ashley. But I admit I did wonder at the time if I knew you as well as I thought I did."

Ashley ran a hand over her eyes. "Everything was such a mess," she began and then stopped at the sound of footsteps on the front stairs.

Kate paused for a moment after the doorbell rang before she walked out of the room to see who was calling on her. She was surprised to see Rosemary Greig standing there, a tentative smile lighting her face.

"Rosemary. Hello." Kate quelled that same irrational guilt as Rosemary's smile widened.

"You look surprised. Can I come in?"

Kate continued to stare at her as her brain seemed to go into slow motion, and Rosemary's smile faltered slightly.

"Unless you're busy or something," she added uncertainly.

"No. No, I'm not busy," Kate said. "But —"

They both turned as Ashley stepped into the hallway.

"Oh, I'm sorry, Kate," Rosemary said quickly. "I was just passing and thought I'd stop in. I didn't realize you had visitors. There was no car."

She started to turn away, and Kate took a step forward. "It's all right, Rosemary. Come on in. It's just an old friend." Just an old friend? Kate could almost laugh hysterically at herself. And why was she asking Rosemary to join them?

"Sure?" Rosemary stepped onto the veranda and smiled at Ashley. "Hello. Hope I'm not intruding."

Ashley shook her head. "No, of course not."

They all returned to the living room and spent a few seconds finding seats before Kate made the introductions.

"So, you work with Kate?" Ashley asked politely,

and Kate got the feeling she wasn't enthusiastic about the interruption.

"Not quite." Rosemary smiled. She was completely at ease, something Kate wished she was. "I'm the lord mayor's personal secretary, but Kate's and my paths cross every so often."

Ashley slid a glance at Kate, and to her consternation Kate felt her cheeks warm with color.

"I don't think we've met before, have we?" Rosemary asked. "Do you live in the Towers?"

"I grew up here but left about ten years ago."

"Oh. And are you back for good or on holiday?"

Kate wanted to know that too.

"I haven't exactly made up my mind. Ostensibly I'm home for my mother's birthday and then to house-sit for my parents when they take an anniversary cruise. But I may decide to stay here."

Kate's heart fluttered as hope soared before she could quash it. So this wasn't just a fleeting visit, Kate thought, and then she rebuked herself again. What did it matter to her what Ashley did or didn't do? But if Ashley did decide to stay, how was Kate going to cope with seeing her all the time?

"It's hard to stay away from the old hometown, isn't it?" Rosemary was saying easily.

Kate couldn't prevent herself from comparing the two women. While they were both shorter than Kate, Ashley had a fuller figure. Rosemary, on the other hand, was slim and small boned, and in her cool cotton dress she looked neat and fresh. Seeing the two women together Kate tried to examine her feelings, but she was having difficulty even keeping up with the conversation.

"Actually, Kate and I went to school together and

were best friends," Ashley said. Rosemary's eyes met and held Kate's, speculation in their depths.

Kate looked away, not wanting Rosemary to suspect the truth behind those words.

"It's ten years since we saw each other," Ashley continued.

"You must have lots to talk about. And here I am barging in on you," Rosemary remarked ruefully.

"That's okay." Kate found her voice. "It's not as though Ashley's leaving tomorrow, are you?"

"No." Ashley gave a wry smile. "That I'm not. We have plenty of time to get reacquainted."

Did Kate imagine the heavy significance of Ashley's tone? She glanced at Rosemary again, saw that same supposition, and decided she hadn't.

Ashley seemed to be subtly warning the other woman off. If she was, Kate reflected, it would mean ... Kate swallowed. Did Ashley want to pick up their relationship where they had left off? Kate felt a fever of elation she had great difficulty subduing.

"Do you see much difference in the town?" Rosemary was asking politely, and Ashley shook her head.

"Not too much, really. But it seemed strange to see the Country Music Statue when we drove into town. I didn't realize country music had taken such a hold. But then again, we used to enjoy the bush dances, didn't we, Kate?"

"Country music's proved to be quite a tourist drawing card." Kate was trying to relax, but somehow her body just grew more tense.

"Country music, plus the local architecture and the gold mining heritage," Rosemary added. "In fact, tourism is a flourishing industry now."

"And have you been living here long yourself?" Ashley asked her, and Rosemary chuckled.

"I'm a newcomer. Been here just a couple of years. I was tired of the city, so I wanted to try country life again. I applied for the job as personal secretary to the lord mayor, and here I am. But I was originally a small-town girl."

"Me too. Well" — Ashley stood up — "I guess I should be heading home."

Kate pushed herself to her feet, trying to decide if she was happy or sad. "It's dark outside now. I'll drive you home," Kate heard herself say.

"No, you won't. You have a guest. I'll just go out the back way and slip through the fence. If I can still fit," she added with a laugh. Kate automatically ran her eyes over Ashley's body. If it had changed at all, it was only for the better, she reflected wryly and glanced across to catch Rosemary doing exactly the same.

"I'll just take the flashlight so Ashley can see where she's going," Kate told Rosemary, and the other woman nodded and relaxed back in her seat. "I won't be long. You can put the TV on if you like."

"Sure." Rosemary smiled, and guilt gnawed away at Kate again.

"I should be able to see all right," Ashley said as they walked through the kitchen to the back door.

"The back light's out." Kate took the flashlight from the cupboard. "I've been meaning to replace the bulb." She walked ahead of Ashley, lighting the steps with the flashlight.

They walked down the cement path to the clothesline and then moved carefully over the lawn toward the back fence, the pool of light dancing on the ground ahead of them. Kate imagined she could feel the heat from Ashley's body as she walked beside her. She swallowed nervously, unwillingly acknowledging Ashley was still as attractive as she always had been.

Had been, Kate reminded herself. Past.

They were under the canopy of the tamarind tree now, and Ashley stopped, putting a warm hand on Kate's arm. Kate had to stop herself from flinching away. Her nerve endings sent a searing message to the pit of her stomach, and she caught back a low moan, wanting only to lean into the softness of Ashley's body. The intensity of her feelings frightened Kate.

"Can I just climb up and check out the tree house?" Ashley was saying, and Kate pulled herself together.

"It's too dark to see anything." She swung the arc of light from the flashlight onto the ladder, and Ashley laughed.

"I reckon I could find my way up there blindfolded." With that she took hold of the ladder and began to climb.

Kate shone the torch on the tree and tried not to watch Ashley's smooth legs moving upward.

"Come on up for a minute, too, Kate," Ashley said as she climbed onto the platform.

Kate hovered uncertainly. With a sigh she slung the strap of the flashlight around her neck and fumbled her way up the tree. She pushed herself up onto the platform and set the light on the old packing case. It bathed them in a circle of unnatural light.

Ashley took the flashlight and shone it around, giving the flooring a tap with the toe of her shoe.

"You've done some work on it," she said easily and replaced the light on the box.

"Yes." Kate swallowed to clear her throat. "I came up here once, and one of the boards almost gave way beneath me, so I had someone look at it."

"It looks like it's held up pretty well." In the dim light Kate saw her quick smile, one that took Kate back in time and caught her somewhere in the chest. "We must have been reasonable tradesmen then," Ashley continued.

"You were, you mean."

Ashley shrugged easily. "You helped me with the extension. New seat, too."

"Packing cases don't do a lot for aging backs."

"You come up here often then?"

"No." Kate shook her head. "Not often. Sometimes to read. Or . . ." She stopped.

"Or?" Ashley raised her eyebrows.

"Usually to read." Kate took a few careful steps over to the railings, needing their support. What would Ashley say if she told her she often came here to remember? And how much those memories hurt.

Ashley sat down on the new chair, testing it out. And then she stood up to subside onto the floor, tanned legs crossed. "This is more like it. Remember the first time I found you here?" she asked softly.

Kate's stomach tensed, twisted painfully, and a pain settled around her heart.

Ashley laughed. "I thought you were going to push

me off the ladder. And then you ordered me off your private property."

Kate pulled a face. "You took me by surprise."

"Well, I wasn't exactly expecting anyone to be in my own, personally-constructed tree house." She sighed, and Kate studied her shadowy profile, feeling the familiar quickening in the pit of her stomach again, the pull that slithered lower to her crotch.

Superficially, Kate supposed Ashley had barely changed. Kate knew her eyes were still that incredible blue, her hair was still shot with pure gold, and freckles still danced across her small nose. Yet underneath there was a subtle change, a tenseness in the way she held herself, and the ready humor that had danced in her eyes had dulled somehow.

"Can you believe it was eighteen years ago, Kate? Time flies, doesn't it?"

Does it? Kate wanted to cry bitterly. Each year of the last ten had been an agony for her without Ashley. "I suppose it does," she said evenly.

"We got into some fine scrapes, didn't we? And it was years before anyone discovered our hideaway."

Kate's fingers tightened on the smooth railing. Scrapes? Is that what Ashley called them? Did she remember it all? The kisses? The —

"I told Jenny about some of them. We rolled around the floor laughing." Ashley smiled and looked up at Kate. "Remember when we let the tires down on Baden's old car? And he blamed Tim?"

Reluctantly, Kate smiled. "It must have been your idea."

Ashley laughed. "Most probably. You were always a goody-two-shoes."

"You certainly got me into a parcel of trouble over the years." And the last time was a doozy.

Something flickered across Ashley's face, and she looked away.

"And your aunt always used to say, 'Just because Ashley Maclean jumps off a bridge, you don't have to follow her, Kate Ballantyne.' "

Kate laughed lightly at Ashley's imitation of her aunt's censorious tones.

"I think your aunt had me pegged right from the start," Ashley remarked dryly.

Kate grew hot at the implication in those words. Kate would have followed Ashley anywhere.

Ashley pushed herself to her feet and dusted her shorts. "I guess we'd better go."

"I guess so." Kate shone the light over the edge of the platform. "I'll go first and shine the light for you." She began the climb downward, adjusting the light as Ashley followed her.

On the last step Kate stumbled, but she quickly recovered herself, grateful that Ashley didn't have to reach out to her. She knew she was fearful of her reaction to Ashley's touch, no matter how innocent.

Kate went to walk toward the fence, but when she turned the light Ashley was still standing at the foot of the ladder, her hand resting on the tree trunk. Kate paused, waiting.

"So, is Rosemary the friend you're seeing on a casual basis?" Ashley asked softly.

Kate caught her breath. "I — What makes you think that?" she hedged, and in the dim light she saw Ashley smile crookedly.

"If she isn't she wants to be," she said evenly.

"You're mistaken," Kate began, and Ashley gave a throaty laugh and took a step toward Kate.

"And you never could tell a lie, Kate," she said, her lowered voice pouring over Kate like warm honey. Kate felt all the fine hairs on her arms rise in anticipation.

"That was a long time ago." Kate fought for some semblance of control of the conversation. "I've changed."

"Have you?"

The two words whispered about inside Kate's head, unlocking doors she thought were secured forever. Her body reacted instantaneously to Ashley's tone, and Kate's nipples hardened beneath her thin T-shirt.

Ashley moved closer still, and she slowly reached out, her fingers running over Kate's arm with practiced ease. Kate swayed toward her, terrified and exhilarated by her body's arousal.

"Kate?" Her hoarsely spoken name danced about in the electricity that arced between them. "Oh, Kate."

And then Ashley closed the remaining distance between them, and her soft, so familiar mouth met Kate's.

CHAPTER SIX

Kate's emotions were tinder dry and as Ashley's lips brushed hers, drew back, touched again, tasted, withdrew only to return, Kate felt the spark take hold, the fire begin to race through her tense body.

Deep inside Kate something broke and, with a heady moan, her arms slid around Ashley's warm body, crushing her to her. Kate's breasts tingled where they pressed against the softness of Ashley's, and their hips strained to mesh together.

Ashley's hands molded Kate's buttocks as she slid

her lips along Kate's jawline to tease her earlobe. "Oh, Kate. You taste so wonderful, just like I remembered."

Remembered. The word echoed in Kate's consciousness, and she slowly came back to the present. And with that consciousness came the pain. With a cry she pushed Ashley away, put some space between them.

"Kate?" Ashley appealed softly, and Kate clutched at the tree trunk, using the sharpness of the bark on her palm to defuse the almost overwhelming hunger to turn back into that so erotic embrace.

Kate straightened, fought to control her breathing before slowly turning back to Ashley. "You'd better go," she said with some small semblance of coolness and bent to retrieve the flashlight from the ground where she'd let it fall.

"Kate, we have to talk about this," Ashley began, her voice thin with the first sign of uncertainty.

"Not now, Ashley. I need time to" — Kate drew a deep breath — "I need some time."

Silence held them for a long moment, and then Ashley moved. "All right. I . . . good night, Kate." She slipped between the loose palings as she had a hundred times before, and she was swallowed up by the darkness.

On shaky legs Kate walked back across the lawn and up the steps. She replaced the flashlight on the cupboard and ran her hand agitatedly through her hair.

"Kate?"

She looked up, startled, and only then did she remember that Rosemary was waiting for her.

"Oh. Rosemary. Sorry I took so long." Kate's face

felt hot with guilty embarrassment. "Ashley . . . we were looking at the tree house we built years ago."

"It's great to have friends who go way back, isn't it?" Rosemary remarked. Kate nodded.

"Yes. So, would you like a cup of coffee or tea?"

"Coffee would be nice, but only if you're having one."

"I think I will." Kate decided it would give her something to do while she pulled herself together. "Did you enjoy your weekend away?" she asked as she spooned the coffee grounds into the percolator.

"It was pretty good. Wish you could have come too. We went up the Broughton. Anne and Tom have a shack up there. No mod cons, but very relaxing."

"That's good." Kate leaned her hip against the countertop as she waited for the coffee to perk.

Rosemary gave Kate an amusing rundown on the highlights of the weekend, and then she strolled over to stand in front of Kate. Kate stiffened.

"How about a kiss hello?" Rosemary took Kate's hand in hers.

Panic rose inside Kate, and she automatically turned her face so that Rosemary's kiss landed on her warm cheek. Rosemary drew back and raised her eyebrows.

Kate's laugh was a little embarrassed. "Sorry. I guess I'm tired."

Rosemary made no comment but gave Kate a level look before graciously moving slightly away. At that moment the percolator wheezed and Kate gratefully turned to occupy herself with pouring coffee into mugs, adding milk and sugar, and offering Rosemary some Anzac biscuits.

They returned to the living room, and Rosemary

sat in the chair Ashley had been sitting in such a short time ago.

"Did you get your work finished?" she asked, and Kate blinked, momentarily forgetting she'd used some unfinished work as the excuse for not going away with the other woman.

"Oh, yes. I wrapped it up last night, so I went for a drive this morning, out along the Townsville road."

"Did you know your friend Ashley was coming home?" Rosemary asked casually, and Kate's reply was equally as offhand.

"I read something about her mother's birthday party in the local paper."

"Where's she been living?"

"Melbourne."

"Working down there?"

"No." Kate swallowed. "Her husband does." There, she'd said it so easily. *Her husband.* "He's a heart surgeon."

Rosemary held Kate's gaze. "Is she the one?"

"The one?" Kate repeated, her mouth drying. "Who?"

"The one who chose a guy and broke your heart," she elaborated gently.

For some reason Kate felt tears well up behind her eyes, and she fought to control them. She struggled to find a nonchalant denial, but her mind was completely blank. Rosemary continued to look at Kate, her expression filled with a knowing sympathy.

"I see she is," she said softly, and Kate cleared her throat.

"It's over," Kate said flatly, wishing she believed the statement.

"Is it? Not for her I'll warrant. She very subtly warned me off."

"You're mistaken," Kate said quickly with little conviction. Hadn't she sensed that too? And hadn't Ashley said the same thing of Rosemary?

"I don't think so." Rosemary grimaced. "And has her husband the doctor come with her?"

Kate shook her head. "She tells me they're divorcing."

"Aha!"

Kate made a negating movement with her head. "There's no aha. I told you before, she made her choice years ago."

"Maybe she's changed her mind."

"Rosemary, you don't understand."

"I guess I don't."

"It's been ten years since, well, since I've seen her."

"Perhaps it's taken her that long to realize she only thought she was straight." Rosemary raised her eyebrows again. "Not feasible?"

Kate sighed. "All I know is that I just don't want to go through it all again."

"Now that I can understand." Rosemary laughed softly. "Anyway, I don't know why I'm defending her cause. Maybe I'm just a sucker for a happy ending. I mean, I live in hope of mine." Her level gaze held Kate's again until Rosemary shrugged and drained her coffee mug. "I'd better be going."

They both stood up, and Rosemary walked across to stand close to Kate.

"Unless you'd like me to stay the night?" she asked lightly.

"I'm pretty tired," Kate put in quickly. "And I have a lot to do at work tomorrow."

Rosemary shrugged exaggeratedly. "Now why did I know you were going to say that? But it's okay, Kate." She crossed to the door. "Will I see you for lunch tomorrow?"

"Of course." Kate walked across the carpet and kissed Rosemary lightly. "And thanks, Rosemary."

"For what, exactly?" Rosemary asked.

Kate shrugged. "For listening maybe. For the advice."

Rosemary rolled her eyes expressively. "Well, I have warned you. I haven't got such a good track record myself when it comes to old loves," she said dryly. She shook her head, went to walk away, and turned back. "Kate, just be careful. As much as I love a happy ending, I have to admit it's sometimes not a good idea to try to turn back the clock. It doesn't always work terribly well."

"I have no intention of doing that," Kate told her, wishing she believed herself. One touch of Ashley's lips, and ten years had disappeared in an instant.

"I don't want to see you get hurt." Rosemary touched Kate's mouth with one finger and held it up to show Kate. "She wears a very becoming shade of lipstick."

Kate flushed at the sight of the smear of pink on Rosemary's finger.

"Subtle and unpretentious, but it doesn't suit your coloring."

Kate rubbed at her lips and Rosemary laughed softly.

"I think I'd better exit before I throw discretion to

the wind and overstate my case." Rosemary walked out onto the veranda, and Kate followed her. "See you tomorrow?"

Kate nodded and could only stand and watch as Rosemary walked out to her car and drove away.

Fortunately for Kate, the next two days at work were so busy she barely had time to think. Getting a selection of books and a display ready for loan to one of the local schools and then going over the final estimates for next year's budget meant Kate had little time during the day to dwell on Ashley and that kiss.

The nights were the problem. Once Kate slipped into bed, those few erotic moments when Ashley's mouth had been on hers replayed over and over in Kate's mind. And she taunted herself with the knowledge that not only had she allowed Ashley to kiss her but she'd returned the kiss in kind. So much for being cool and withdrawn. One touch of Ashley's lips on hers, and all Kate's resolve had fallen apart.

Kate spent Monday night tossing and turning, and when Tuesday night promised more of the same she switched on her reading lamp and reached in desperation for her copy of *Gold Fever*.

Gradually she calmed as she became involved in the story. The characters came alive, and she could almost hear the sounds of picks on shale, of rushing water in crude makeshift sluices, the jangle of horse bridles, the heat and the buzz of insects.

Kate became engrossed in the plight of Clare Darby, and she could identify with the strangeness the heroine felt as she tried to fit in with her new family.

Clare moved into the rough shack that her uncle had built on his mining lease. Her aunt, Clare's mother's sister, quietly welcomed her niece's help with the daily chores as she cooked and washed for her husband and his two brothers, who had pitched their tent nearby.

Her three uncles worked the mine from daylight till dusk, convinced they would find the mother lode. That Clare's aunt had given up any hope of that happening was apparent to her young niece.

Kate could feel the young woman's sadness as she pined for her parents and the other life she'd led in Brisbane. Then Clare met Tess, who, she learned, was the daughter of a shopkeeper in the township. Tess was to marry Clare's youngest uncle as soon as Caleb had enough gold to buy a cattle property. Tess was Clare's age, and she visited regularly. Soon Clare began looking forward to the young woman's visits.

More often than not the two young women met in the shade of a cluster of trees by the shallow creek. The heat danced about them as they clasped hands.

Kate turned the page to read on, and suddenly she stilled. Turning back a page she reread the few paragraphs and her blood ran ice in her veins.

As Tess pressed a passionate kiss on Clare's lips Kate grew hot all over. She studied the dialogue with an ominous sense of déjà vu. The impassioned exchange between the two young women seemed so true to life, was so familiar . . .

Kate gasped, her fingers pressed to her lips, as the unbelievable truth dawned.

She read on into the early hours of the morning, not stopping until she'd turned the last page. And then she lay in the dark, a myriad thoughts chasing each other busily in her mind. She yearned for the oblivion of sleep, but no matter how hard she tried she was unable to slip over into unconsciousness.

She was almost relieved when dawn flooded her room with light and she could climb from her bed and occupy her mind with fixing herself some breakfast and getting ready for work.

On Wednesday afternoon Kate was walking back to the library desk after helping an elderly borrower choose some books when Ryan's storytelling group burst from the activities room. Twenty or thirty youngsters scrambled to the desk to have their loans processed.

Kate began to scan their books into the computer, her mind running on habit, the various children's faces not really registering until a familiar voice claimed her attention.

"Hi, Kate! How are you?"

And even as Kate's gaze settled on Jennifer Andrews's smiling face, her body tensed as she wondered if Ashley was here with her daughter. But Jenny was looking at her expectantly.

"Oh, hello, Jen. Did you enjoy the storytelling session?" she asked with far more equanimity than she was feeling.

"It was excellent." Jenny beamed.

"Is your mother with you?" Kate was horrified to hear herself ask the child.

Jenny shook her head. "No, Gran wanted her to help her with some stuff for the party, so Aunt Belinda dropped us off. Oh." She drew forward a young boy of about her own age. "This is my cousin,

Josh." Jen made the introductions. "He's a few months older than me."

"Nice to meet you, Josh." Kate gravely took his politely extended hand.

"Josh hasn't read many books, but I've given him some suggestions." Jenny indicated the books her cousin clutched under his arm, and Josh rolled his eyes eloquently.

"I just haven't read the same books Jenny's read," he said resignedly, and Kate hid a smile.

"I loved the books on the history of the gold mining around here that Ryan picked out for me last weekend. They were cool, weren't they, Josh?"

"They were interesting," Josh conceded.

"Mum told me about the old Eureka mine and that you both played out there sometimes, looking for gold," Jenny said, her face alight with excitement.

"Not in the mine," Kate said quickly. "It's all boarded up because it's not safe. But we did look for gold in the mullock heaps."

"Josh and I are going fossicking one day." Jenny's blue eyes grew large. "We might even find a really big nugget."

"What's this? Another case of the dreaded gold fever?" A woman's voice broke in, and Kate looked up to find herself facing Ashley's sister, Belinda.

Kate assessed the smiling woman who had her arm around Jenny's shoulder. She'd gained a few pounds, but she scarcely looked her thirty-five years.

"Hello, Kate. Long time no see. Are these two asking for treasure maps?"

Kate smiled back at her. "If we had any of those we'd all be out trying our luck."

"Isn't that the truth." Belinda brushed a strand of

Jenny's hair back from her face. "You'll have to ask Uncle Tim to take you out. He used to go panning for gold himself years ago, didn't he, Kate? Or was that Baden?"

"Tim, I think. He found some, too. If I remember rightly he kept it in a small vial, and none of us were allowed to so much as breathe on it. And he wouldn't tell us where he got it."

"That's right. He was a real pain about it." She laughed. "I wonder if he ever got it assayed."

"Do you think he's still got it, Aunt Belinda?" Jenny asked, obviously fascinated.

"You'll have to ask him when he arrives on Friday night." Belinda looked back at Kate. "And talking of the weekend, are you coming to Mum's birthday party on Saturday night, Kate?"

Kate paused. Surely Belinda remembered the dissension between herself and Ashley when Ashley got married? Patsy Maclean may not have told her elder daughter everything, but Belinda must have been surprised when Kate didn't attend Ashley's wedding.

"The party?" she repeated banally. "Oh, no. I don't think so. I wasn't planning on coming."

"Well, feel free to," Belinda said lightly. "The noise will probably keep you awake anyway so, as they say, if you can't beat 'em, join 'em. I'm sure Mum would be pleased to see you."

Kate wasn't so sure about that. And now that Ashley was home and not safely the length of the continent away, Kate was convinced Patsy Maclean would be less than pleased to see Kate.

"Well, kiddos. If you've chosen your books, we'd best get back home to the whirlwind of preparations. See you later, Kate."

The next afternoon Kate walked back through the doors of the library and sighed. Phillip was a pain in the derriere. His penny-pinching meant she would have to redo the majority of the budget. If she could see any advantage in what he'd suggested she wouldn't mind. But as Kate saw it, it was all simply a convoluted way of making more work for her.

Walking over to the desk, Kate gave Ryan a rueful grin. "I'd kill for a cup of coffee. I don't suppose there's one brewed for a librarian who's just been subjected to bureaucratic overkill and who's reached the end of her tether?"

Ryan grinned. "Perking as we speak."

"You're an angel." Kate went to walk through to the staff room but Ryan called her back.

"Kate. Just a minute." He bent forward and lowered his voice. "She's here."

"Who is?" Kate frowned.

"Our author."

Kate stiffened, feeling herself flush, and she glanced quickly around the library. "Leigh Mossman? Where?"

Ryan nodded and motioned his head in the direction of Kate's office. "She came in about fifteen minutes ago and asked to see you."

"I thought she'd ring first," Kate began, and Ryan shook his head.

"Well, she did ring. Not long after you'd left. I told her you'd be back by two. I thought that would give you time to have lunch, but I should have known

Phillip the Pompous would keep you the best part of the day."

Kate half smiled at Ryan's nickname for the town clerk before glancing at the closed door of her office, a sense of foreboding in the pit of her stomach.

"Took me a moment to realize who she was, but I think you'll recognize her too." Ryan grinned. "Shouldn't you go on in and see her?"

Kate continued to stand undecided.

"I'll bring you your coffee and a cup for her too, okay? And how about some of my Mum's cookies?"

Kate took a steadying breath and nodded, making no move to cross to her office.

"You better go in. She's expecting you. I rang Phillip's office, and they said you were on your way back so I told her you'd only be five minutes," Ryan encouraged. "Shall I give you a couple of minutes before I bring in the coffee?"

"What? Oh, the coffee. Yes, please, Ryan." Kate pulled herself together, made herself walk across to the door.

She paused before entering, tried to push the feeling of betrayal from her mind, but her stomach muscles clenched as she remembered the book she'd finished on Tuesday night and hadn't been able to get out of her mind since.

Betrayal. The word flashed before her eyes, and her anger overrode the anticipation of seeing her again. For it had to be her.

Kate pushed open the door and strode purposefully inside.

She was sitting in the easy chair off to the right, leafing through a magazine Ryan must have given her, and she looked up with those incredible blue eyes. A slow smile lit her face, and Kate felt that ever-present quickening of desire.

"Hello, Kate. Did you guess?"

Kate walked around her desk and sat down, her fingers smoothing the lapel of her tailored jacket. She was glad she'd chosen to wear her suit. Somehow it cloaked her in professionalism and put some small barrier between herself, her very vulnerable self, and this so inconceivably attractive woman.

"Did I guess you were Leigh Mossman? Not until Tuesday night, about page one hundred and twenty-five." Kate sat down behind her desk, another small bastion of refuge.

"My agent suggested I take out that subplot or change it, but I held out. I wanted Clare to be attracted to Tess."

Kate looked at Ashley's smiling face, let her eyes wander over Ashley's body. She wore a silk shirt tucked into a pair of white tailored slacks, and the azure color of her blouse reflected the bright blue of her eyes.

"Why did you do it, Ash?" Kate was amazed at the evenness of her tone.

"I wanted to write about the power of women's love —"

"Not just that. The whole thing. Why did you put it in the book? All the things we said to each other, and did, for all the world to read. What point were you trying to make?"

"No point. At least, not the way you mean it. I just . . ." Ashley shrugged. "I suppose I just wanted you to know how much I treasured what we had."

Kate bit off an exclamation of disbelief. "Oh. right. And you'll tell the truth to your grandchildren."

"Yes, I will, if you want to tell them. As long as you're there to tell them too."

Kate stood up. "Stop this, Ashley. I can't take much more of it. How can you expect to come home and just pick up where you left off as though nothing had happened."

"This isn't the first time I've been home looking for you."

Kate watched the play of emotions flicker across Ashley's face.

"The first time I came back Jenny hadn't even been born. My mother wouldn't help me, and all your aunt would say was that you'd gone to Brisbane. I was distraught. I pleaded with her to tell me where you were, but she sent me away. I searched the Brisbane directory for a phone number, but you weren't listed.

"Then my parents called the doctor and a social worker. They convinced me to go back to Dean. They told me marriage took time and patience and working together."

Ashley sighed. "They thought they were doing the right thing, but they didn't know Dean. My parents are normal, loving people. They couldn't know how possessive, how controlling Dean could be. When he came home every day he'd cross-examine me. Who had been there? Whom did I see? Whom had I talked to? What did they say? Was I attracted to the guy next door?"

She shook her head. "It went on and on until finally I made it worse by telling him I didn't love him, that I loved someone else. He never forgave me for that."

"You told Dean about us?" Kate asked in disbelief, and Ashley gave a short, humorless laugh.

"Oh, no, I didn't make that big a mistake. No specific names or gender were mentioned. I knew Dean by then. He'd have gone ballistic if I'd told him I was in love with a woman. Anyway, it doesn't matter any more. Dean's someone else's problem now."

In love with a woman? Did that mean . . . ? Kate forced the wildly electrifying thoughts from her mind and absently played with the paperweight on her desk, but before she could comment there was a soft tap on the door and Ryan stuck his head into Kate's office.

"Ready for coffee?" he asked brightly, blushing when Ashley turned her smile on him.

"Coffee would be wonderful," she said, and Ryan came inside, setting down the tray on Kate's desk before turning eagerly back to Ashley.

"I can't believe you're Leigh Mossman. I mean, your brothers played football with my brother, and I think Tim used to go out with my sister way back."

"It's a close-knit little town, isn't it?" Ashley said with a soft laugh.

Ryan blushed again. "Yes. You can't say anything about anyone in case they're related."

They laughed together, but Ryan sobered when he glanced across at his boss. "Looks like you can use the coffee too, Kate." He turned back to Ashley. "As well as haggling over the budget all morning, Kate was up all night on Tuesday reading your book. That's why she still looks so seedy. I warned her not to start *Gold Fever* at night because she wouldn't be able to put it down."

"So my book kept you awake?" Ashley turned back to Kate, the tone of her voice setting Kate's nerve endings jangling. Kate tried to relax back into her chair, aware of Ryan's interested presence.

"You write very well," she said flatly, and Ashley laughed.

"Remember I used to say when I was at school that I was going to be a writer one day?" She turned back to Ryan. "But no one believed me except Kate. She always had faith in me."

Ryan looked from one to the other.

"Kate and I were best friends at school," Ashley explained.

"Hey, that's great. I didn't know that. I was a long way behind you guys but, as I said, I do remember my brother playing football with Tim." Ryan passed Ashley the sugar. "The locals are sure going to be surprised at the Meet the Author afternoon we've got planned. It's going to be really popular."

Ashley pulled a face. "We hope."

"Oh, it will be. As I said, we all loved the book. And Mum's especially excited. She can't wait to meet you."

"Well, that's one person who'll be here," Ashley teased.

"One person? Loads of people have booked in to come along and hear you read from *Gold Fever*," Ryan enthused. "There'll only be standing room, you'll see."

"Now you're starting to make me nervous." Ashley feigned concern.

"Don't be. Everyone will hang on your every word,

no matter what you talk about. You're a local girl turned famous and, besides, we don't get many writers here, do we, Kate?"

"No, we don't," Kate said evenly, and Ryan shifted a little uncomfortably at Kate's apparent lack of enthusiasm.

"Well, I'd better get ready for the Eventide ladies." He rubbed his hands nervously together. "They'll be here any minute."

"I'll come out and give you a hand." Kate went to get up, but Ryan waved her back into her seat.

"No. Don't worry, Kate. The old ladies will be over the moon having me to themselves." He grinned. "Really, I can manage. I'll buzz you if I need you."

"He looks very much like his brother," Ashley said as the young man closed the door behind him. "He must have been just a kid when I left. Makes you feel old, doesn't it?"

Kate smiled faintly. "Just a little."

Ashley's level gaze held Kate's. "You haven't said whether you actually liked my book or not?"

Kate shrugged. "You don't need me to tell you how great it is. The critics have done that."

Ashley grimaced. "But I'd like you to tell me you enjoyed it."

"I did enjoy it. But I still think you could have left that part out of it."

"Are you ashamed of our relationship, Kate?" Ashley asked, and Kate stood up, paced the floor beside her desk.

"Shame's got nothing to do with it. I just didn't want it written down and bandied about."

"No one knows the truth except you and me."

"And your mother," Kate put in exasperatedly.

"She didn't tell anyone else, Kate. I know she threatened to at the time, but she didn't."

"And that makes it okay."

"Kate, for heaven's sake. I wanted it, Clare's and Tess's relationship, I wanted it to be a sort of tribute, if you like, to us."

"By making Tess marry Clare's uncle and Clare end up with the hero. Well, it's about true to life."

"It had to be that way, Kate. When I decided to write *Gold Fever*, it was with the idea of making a career for myself, a way of becoming independent and being able to support Jen and myself, so I could divorce Dean. I mean, I had no salable qualifications except my writing. I had to give the book mainstream appeal." Ashley stood up and moved closer to Kate. Kate tensed, a surge of raw emotion clutching at her stomach muscles.

"I feel betrayed," Kate got out thickly before she could pull back the deep-seated pain of the words.

"Oh, Kate. Do you think I don't know that? But I didn't mean it to be that way, and I'm sorry. Back then I had the most diabolical familial pressure put on me to marry Dean and —"

"I meant by what you included in the book," Kate exclaimed angrily.

"Because Clare had to give up Tess?"

"Because of the words you used. What you and I said to each other. It was us, Ash, and it should have stayed just between us."

"I guess it was about us, but you and I, well, that was my only experience, Kate."

"Oh, Ashley, for heaven's sake —"

"It was, Kate. But before I decided to write the book I did try."

"Try?" Kate's mouth went dry.

Ashley's lips twisted wryly. "To get more experience. It was sort of twofold, really. It happened a couple of years ago. I was so mixed up. I wanted to prove to myself once and for all that I was straight, that what we had, you and I, was just, well, just something I'd blown up into something more than it actually was."

Kate watched as a wave of pain slid across Ashley's face. She wanted desperately to ask what Ashley had discovered and just as desperately didn't want to know.

"Look, Ashley —"

"I called a gay and lesbian hot line and asked about places I could go," Ashley continued softly. "Eventually I got up the courage, and I went to a club. And I found my answers, Kate. I met some really nice women there. But when it came to the crunch, I couldn't do it. I felt like I was cheating on you somehow."

"Dean was the one you were cheating on," Kate said harshly, and Ashley shook her head.

"Dean had nothing to do with it."

"Ash, this is ridiculous."

"You're the only woman, the only person, I've ever been attracted to, Kate." Ashley's voice dropped impossibly lower. "That's the way it'll always be for me."

"Ash, don't."

"Don't what — don't tell the truth? Because it is the truth, Kate."

"Ash, I think we should, I mean, we shouldn't . . ."

"But I did write the other version. I had to," Ashley finished softly.

"The other version?" Kate repeated, every nuance of her body tuned to the nearness of the other woman's.

"Ten years after they were married, Tess and Clare meet up again in Brisbane. Clare's a widow, and Tess's husband, Caleb, has run out on her and their children. Clare and Tess fall into each other's arms and live happily ever after."

The lowered tone of Ashley's voice poured over Kate, seeking out each tiny chink in her armor, inveigling itself beneath her guard, and Kate fought to hold on to some semblance of control.

Ashley reached out, ran her warm fingertip along the length of Kate's jaw, and paused at the corner of Kate's mouth before continuing to the softness of her trembling lips. Of its own accord, Kate's tongue tip came out, tasted, drew back. Ashley's steady gaze held Kate's as she slowly put the finger Kate had touched with her tongue into her own mouth.

Kate sank back against the edge of her desk as her knees almost gave out on her. Ashley followed her, her legs resting against Kate's, her hands reaching out, drawing Kate into the circle of her arms until they were molded together. And Kate completely lost all control again.

She clutched Ashley to her, and their lips met in a kiss of feverish abandonment.

CHAPTER SEVEN

Kate knew deep down she had been anticipating this moment since that brief kiss they'd shared in the darkness below the tree house. In all honesty her impassioned body had simply been waiting, her whole being needing this nearness, this familiar affinity with all that Ashley had meant to her. And Kate clung to Ashley as though she were drowning.

As Ashley's leg insinuated itself between Kate's, she murmured deep in her throat. Her straight skirt slid upward as Ashley's hand moved over her stocking-clad thigh, the whispering rasp of skin on nylon echoing enticingly about the silent confines of Kate's office.

"Oh, Kate, Kate," Ashley murmured thickly as her lips tenderly played over the curve of Kate's cheek and teased her sensitive earlobe.

Some vaguely rational part deep inside Kate clamored a warning, but she was far beyond all caution. She threw her head back, and Ashley's so satiny lips tantalized the arch of her throat and settled on the wild erotic beat of the pulse that throbbed there at its base.

"Oh, Kate. I've dreamed of this moment for so long," Ashley breathed brokenly. "I've wanted to hold you in my arms, wanted to feel the strength of you, your softness."

The satiny, sensual sound of Ashley's voice, the obvious arousal in the way the words caught in the other woman's throat, sent a spreading fire raging through Kate, and she pulled Ashley impossibly closer. She fancied she said Ashley's name, but she couldn't be sure if she'd actually spoken it or if she simply repeated it like a litany in her mind.

"Oh, Kate, I love you. I've never stopped loving you."

Kate slid one hand upward over Ashley's hips, her narrow waist, to mold the full curve of her breast, and another frisson of pure desire shuddered through her as Ashley's hardened nipple thrust against her palm.

The entire room seemed to vibrate with the electricity that sparked in the air around them, between them. And then the belligerent sound of the buzzer struck them both like a blow, bringing them so harshly back to earth.

Ashley lifted her head, her blue eyes still burning bright with arousal, and her gaze met and compellingly held Kate's.

For a few seconds Kate was completely paralyzed, and then awareness dawned. In horror she realized just how they would look to even the most casual observer. Their clothing in disarray. Their lips swollen and so obviously kissed. They looked as though they'd been making love on Kate's desk. Which, she acknowledged ashamedly, they had been.

Kate pushed Ashley away, and her trembling hands slipped her skirt back into place and straightened her jacket. Somehow she managed to step around her desk before she fell into her chair.

"Kate . . ."

There was a brief tap on her office door before it opened, and Phillip Walker stepped into the room.

At the back of her sluggish mind Kate realized Ryan must have buzzed her as a warning that Phillip was heading toward her office, and she made a mental note to thank him profusely. If he hadn't . . .

"Kate, I thought you could use these notes I made on the budget changes." He stopped, adjusting his heavy glasses as Ashley walked around and sat down in the other chair. "Why, Ashley Maclean, isn't it?" Phillip held out his hand, and Ashley made a perfunctory move to shake it.

"Hello, Phillip. You don't seem to have changed much." Ashley's voice was amazingly normal, and only Kate was aware of the paleness of her face.

"Well, thank you." Phillip beamed. "I might say the same of you. It must be, what? Ten years or more? So what have you been doing with yourself? Certainly not living in the Towers."

"No. I've been in Melbourne. And doing the usual. Got married. Getting a divorce."

Phillip frowned understandingly. "I'm sorry to hear that. I'm divorced myself."

"It seems Kate was the only sensible one," Ashley said lightly. "Remaining unmarried."

"Yes, well, there's nothing wrong with marriage," Phillip stated earnestly. "You just have to choose the right person. I can't see myself not getting married again." He glanced pointedly at Kate, but she made herself fix her attention on the notes he'd given her.

"Thanks for these, Phillip," she said quickly. "I'll go over them as soon as I can. Oh, by the way, Ashley's our visiting writer for our Meet the Author afternoon next week."

"Author?" Phillip blinked at Ashley in amazement.

"Don't tell me you haven't read my book, Phillip?" Ashley said with a smile, and Phillip coughed, obviously disconcerted.

"Well, no I haven't as yet. But I intend to. It seems to have taken the literary world by storm."

"Perhaps not quite by storm." Ashley laughed lightly. "Let's just say it has rippled the surface of the pond."

"By what Kate's told me, you're being modest." Phillip put his hands in his pockets and rocked slightly on the heels of his highly polished shoes. "Actually, romances are not my books of choice, but seeing as you wrote it, Ashley, I'll read it for sure."

"Why, thank you, Phillip." Ashley inclined her head.

"You know, it always amazes me where writers get

their ideas. I believe yours is set in the Towers. Is it biographical?"

Kate tensed. If Phillip only knew the truth.

"Not all of it," Ashley was saying patiently. "But I guess you subconsciously pick up bits and pieces of people and situations. It's all grist for the mill. So you never know, Phillip, you might see yourself in one of the characters," Ashley teased.

"Have you put me in the book?" he asked, taking her seriously.

Ashley grinned. "I'll never tell."

He adjusted his glasses again and smiled at her. "You always were something of a tease, Ashley. Well, fancy you writing a book. Maybe we could get together over dinner one evening and you could tell me all about it."

Ashley all but blanched, and Kate had to hide an involuntary smile. Ashley's teasing had often landed her in trouble in the past.

"Oh, I'll be as busy as a bee in clover for the next few weeks, Phillip, house-sitting for my parents. And I have a young daughter I couldn't leave."

"You have a daughter? Well, maybe Kate could babysit," Phillip said easily, and Kate looked at him in amazement. Phillip really was the limit.

"We'll see," Ashley said noncommittally and glanced at her wristwatch. "Well, Kate, I suppose we should talk about what you want me to do at the Meet the Author afternoon."

"And I should be getting back to work, too. This is a hectic time at the moment for those of us in local government." Phillip pursed his lips importantly. "Get back to me tomorrow on the budget, Kate. Nice to see you again, Ashley." He turned and walked out the door.

Ashley gave a strangled laugh. "My God! You said he hadn't changed, and he hasn't, has he?"

"I'm afraid not," Kate agreed. They continued to look at each other, and Kate found herself flushing now that they were alone again. She rubbed at the start of a headache between her eyes. "About next week, I think if you just tell everyone how you got the idea for the book, how you wrote it, and maybe read out a passage or two."

"How about page one hundred and twenty?" Ashley said softly, and Kate's mouth dried.

"Ashley, I'm pretty busy now and —"

"We should talk, Kate. Don't you think? But you're right. Your office isn't exactly, well . . ." She grimaced. "Wrong place, wrong time. The story of my life." Ashley stood up. "And I have to pick Jenny and Josh up from the movies soon. But I think we do have to talk."

Kate shook her head. "Talking won't change anything. You can't wipe out ten years with a snap of your fingers," she said, and Ashley made a negating movement with her hand.

"I know. I wouldn't even attempt to try to do that. But I want to know what you feel, Kate. I want to know about you, what you've been doing all these years."

Kate gave an exclamation of disbelief. "All of a sudden you care about what I've been doing since you left." Kate only just prevented herself from saying *left me.* "That's pretty rich."

"I've always cared."

Kate broke in on her, her voice angrily low. "Oh, yes. You cared so much that you couldn't even face me. You just rang me to invite me to your wedding."

"It wasn't like that, Kate, and you know it." Ashley ran her hand through her hair. "There was so much more going on than you knew about."

"And I thought you told me everything," Kate put in sarcastically.

Ashley's looked away, her lashes dark slashes on her pale face. "I was under enormous pressure from everyone back then. My mother. Dean." She looked at Kate again. "Even you."

"Me?" Kate sat back in her chair. "Look, Ashley, I don't care to talk about this now."

"Don't I get the chance to tell you my side of it?" Ashley appealed, and Kate sighed.

"What good would that do after all this time? It's passed, Ashley."

"I've missed you."

Kate ran a shaky hand over her eyes. "I've missed you, too, Ash," she said flatly. "But as I said, I got over it. I've put all that behind me. And I don't want to go through it all again."

"I guess I'd better go then." Ashley walked over to the door. She paused, her hand resting on the door knob, and she looked back at Kate. "You say you put it all behind you, but have you, Kate?"

"Yes," Kate said with more conviction than she felt.

Ashley's full lips quirked. "I don't think you have, Kate, any more than I have. That kiss was" — she paused — "pretty incredible, didn't you think?" Her voice dropped impossibly lower. "So much so that I want to do it again. And I know you do, too."

"You don't *know* anything about me now, Ash. We're different people." Kate gave a faint, humorless smile. "We don't know each other at all any more. Now, please, I have work to do."

For a long moment Ashley continued to gaze at Kate, and then she sighed. "We'd know each other anywhere at any time, Kate. It doesn't matter how many years we've been apart. It's been that way since the moment we met. That will never change."

And then she was gone, the door closing behind her with a mocking click.

Not until she arrived home did Kate remember it was Thursday and she was to have her usual dinner with Rosemary. She glanced at her wristwatch and groaned. It was too late to beg off, so she forced herself to have a quick shower and changed into a pair of lightweight slacks and a cool cotton blouse.

What was she going to do about Rosemary? she asked herself as she headed across town. In all fairness, she knew she should have told the other woman she had had no right to begin any sort of relationship with anyone.

She suspected there was something missing in her personality. She couldn't seem to let herself get close to anyone.

In the beginning she'd thought it was just that she'd been hurt so badly by Ashley. Time would heal all wounds, she told herself. But the passing of time made no difference. Perhaps Ashley's perfidy had left her with incurable emotional damage. And now that Ashley was back, she . . .

She what? Kate angrily asked herself. Things hadn't changed. Ashley had broken her young heart, and she'd spent years trying to recover. She had no intention of allowing Ashley to do it again.

Kate frowned. Her relationship with Rosemary had been casual from the start. It had been an unspoken understanding between them. Rosemary knew that. Didn't she? Kate shifted gears guiltily. She hadn't allowed Rosemary to think otherwise. Had she?

Kate battled with herself as she turned into Rosemary's driveway and walked up the steps.

Rosemary carried the conversation through dinner, and Kate tried valiantly to keep her mind focused on the other woman.

"Honestly, Phillip Walker is the most boring man I've ever had the misfortune to meet," Rosemary was saying exasperatedly. "And I hear he had you jumping through hoops over the budget."

Kate nodded. "That about sums it up nicely. I think he was even worse this year than he was last year, if that's possible."

Rosemary gave an exclamation of disgust. "Talk about a classic case of a little power being a dangerous thing. Just between you and me, the lord mayor and Phillip had words this afternoon. The lord mayor is as ticked off with Phillip's pompousness as everyone else is."

"I can believe that." Kate shook her head. "And I'll probably have to go through another session with him tomorrow."

Rosemary took a sip of her coffee. "A little bird also told me you had a visit from our famous local author," she said casually.

Kate stiffened. "Yes." She made herself laugh. "Is

there anything that goes on you don't know about, Rosemary?" she teased. "How do you get your information?"

Rosemary tapped the side of her nose with her forefinger. "Oh, I have my ways." She paused. "So? Are you going to tell me all about it?"

Kate swallowed.

"Well?" Rosemary prompted.

"Actually, it was a huge surprise really." Kate fancied she could hear her own heartbeats thundering in her chest. "Leigh Mossman turned out to be Ashley Andrews."

And what would Rosemary think if Kate told her she'd lost all sense of propriety and kissed Leigh Mossman with uncharacteristic recklessness? That it had happened in her office where anyone could have happened upon them. And that Phillip Walker had almost discovered them.

Rosemary blinked. "Your friend, Ashley Andrews, is Leigh Mossman?"

Kate nodded.

"I see." Rosemary took another sip of her coffee. "And you didn't know?"

"No." Kate kept her eyes on her own coffee cup. That wasn't strictly true, but neither was it a lie. Kate hadn't known until she'd read the book.

"That's interesting." Rosemary paused again. "It does sort of add a new dimension to one part of the book, though. Don't you think?"

Kate turned to look at the other woman.

"Where Clare falls for Tess," Rosemary explained. "Actually I was holding out a faint hope that they'd get together in the end, but I knew it wouldn't happen in a mainstream novel."

"Ashley said that, too. That she had to write for the mass market."

"I guess she had to be realistic about it."

"Yes."

"So has she changed her mind?"

Kate looked across at Rosemary inquiringly. "What do you mean?"

"About being straight. You said she and her husband are divorced. Was that the reason?"

"I have no idea," Kate said, trying to keep the defensiveness out of her voice. "I told you I haven't heard from her for ten years. How would I know?"

"For what it's worth, I think she's one of us, Kate," Rosemary said levelly.

"How can you know that?" Kate began and Rosemary laughed softly.

"I just have the knack of knowing. Maybe it's well-developed gaydar. I picked up on you, didn't I?"

"Rosemary, I . . ." Kate paused.

"Don't worry, it's not that obvious with either of you. And if people were more accepting, we wouldn't be having this conversation. And Ashley's book would have ended with Clare and Tess riding off into the sunset. But even so, it was still a great read," Rosemary said.

She moved closer to Kate and put her lips to the back of Kate's hand. "The love scenes, even the relatively mild one between the lines with Clare and Tess, were very erotic, didn't you think?"

Kate shifted uncomfortably. "I guess they were."

"I suppose it must be strange to read a book written by someone you know." Rosemary grinned. "Especially the love scenes."

"Yes, it is."

"Did you see any characters in the book you recognized?"

"No, of course not. What do you mean?" Kate's voice sounded accusing, and Rosemary raised her eyebrows.

"I'm sorry, Kate. I didn't mean to upset you. Shall we change the subject?" She set her coffee cup down, reached across, and took Kate's hand in hers, turning it over so that her tongue tip could tease Kate's palm.

Shifting uncomfortably, Kate cleared her throat. "Rosemary, look, I, I'm a little tired tonight. I had a pretty wearing time with Phillip, and I think I'd better have an early night."

Rosemary looked at Kate and frowned slightly. "You do look tired."

Kate felt a sliver of relief. Maybe she could leave without raising Rosemary's suspicions. *Coward!* an inner voice jeered at her, demanding she tell Rosemary the truth. Kate knew she should and she wavered, wondering where to start, what to say?

"But are you sure it's just that?"

Rosemary's words seized Kate's attention. "What do you mean?" she asked, her conscience jabbing at her guiltily.

"I mean, Ashley Andrews."

"Ashley?"

Rosemary nodded. "I have a feeling everything comes back to Ashley where you're concerned, Kate," Rosemary said softly.

Kate sighed. "Look, Rosemary, it's not what you think. It's just that I, I mean, we haven't seen each other for ten years. And I'm finding it a little difficult to, well, get used to the fact that she's here."

"Are you still in love with her?"

"No!" Kate stated vehemently, and it was Rosemary's turn to sigh. "Of course I'm not in love with her," Kate repeated. "For heaven's sake, Rosemary, we were just kids when I saw her last."

"Methinks the lady doth protest too much," Rosemary said lightly, and Kate fought to quell the surge of anger that rose inside her.

Kate wanted to deny it again, and she wanted to believe it. Yet somehow she knew she couldn't. She knew she would be deluding herself. If it hadn't been for that kiss this afternoon she may have . . .

"Look, Kate. I think I understand how you feel," Rosemary said moderately. "At least I know how it was with my friend Sue and me. Ashley meant so much to you. She hurt you very much, and now she's back. You're having trouble sorting out your feelings. Right?"

"Something like that," Kate admitted, subdued. "Rosemary, I don't know how to say this —"

Rosemary grimaced. "You think you should take some time out until you can decide how you really feel about Ashley. How's that?"

"I guess that about sums it up." Kate looked at the other woman. "I'm sorry, Rosemary, if I've —"

Rosemary put her fingers lightly on Kate's lips. "You don't have to apologize. As much as I hate to admit it, it's the sensible thing to do." She leaned closer and gently pressed her lips to Kate's. "Just remember one thing, though. I'll be here if you need to talk or anything. Okay?"

"Of course." Kate stood up, pulled Rosemary to her, and hugged her. "And thanks. For everything."

* * * * *

117

The next afternoon after work Kate was drawn again to the tree house, and no matter how much she chastised herself for going down to that sanctuary, she still couldn't seem to stop herself from walking down to the end of the garden.

And yet sitting in the cool, leafy refuge only brought back memories she'd kept at bay for so many years. Each corner of their retreat, hers and Ashley's, held a multitude of memories that seemed to encroach on all Kate's waking moments these days. Or so it seemed.

With nary a blink of her eye, she could picture the two of them, naked in the heat of the northern summer, bodies glistening as they lay together.

They spent so many hours in the tree house, lying side-by-side on a rug, reading or talking, but more often making love. They'd even devised a rope pulley to lift the ladder when they were in the tree house in case Ashley's brothers discovered their hideaway.

Kate could see herself, raising herself on one elbow to kiss Ashley's bare shoulder. Their young bodies were so different. Kate was long and slender, her skin toning slightly olive, whereas Ashley was very fair, her body all softly curving.

When had it all started to go wrong? Kate wondered. With hindsight she supposed it had started the day Ashley had dropped her bombshell.

Lying side-by-side on the rug in the tree house, they'd just made love and Kate was still wrapped in a heady euphoria.

"I suppose we should get dressed," she'd said

118

languidly. "But I can't get enough of the feel of your smooth skin, your incredible breasts."

Ashley gently ran her hand down Kate's arm, her fingers sensually skimming her skin. "Mine are too big. I'd rather they were like yours."

"Mine?" Kate giggled. "I haven't got any worth speaking about."

"They're beautiful," Ashley said and teased one small nipple with her tongue tip.

"Mmm. I'll give you fifty years to stop doing that." With a smile Kate turned and murmured, "I love you, Ash." She looked down at Ashley's face, caught a fleeting expression of pain, and she frowned. "Ash, what's wrong?"

"Oh, nothing." Ashley sighed, lying back, settling Kate's head onto her shoulder. "Just wishing we were the only two people on earth."

Kate laughed softly. "Up here we are. But if we really were, we might get sick and tired of each other."

"I suppose." Ashley looked up at Kate through her eyelashes. Her hand continued to touch Kate's skin, but Kate sensed she wasn't thinking about the feel or texture of it just at that moment.

"You seem very pensive, Ash. Too much love making, do you think?" Kate tried for humor and was rewarded by Ashley's slow smile.

She relaxed back on the rug and snuggled into Ashley's side. "So, are we walking to the movies tomorrow night or is your father or Baden going to drop us in town?"

Ashley was silent for long moments. "That's what I wanted to talk about." She took a deep breath. "I can't go with you tomorrow night."

Kate sat up and turned toward her. "You can't? Why not? I thought you particularly wanted to see this movie."

"I do, but Dean asked me to go with him."

Kate went cold all over.

"And I said I would."

CHAPTER EIGHT

Kate felt as though she had been elbowed in her solar plexus. She looked down at Ashley, but the other girl wouldn't meet her gaze. "I don't understand." Kate swallowed painfully. "Why, Ash?"

Ashley sat up too and pulled on her T-shirt.

For once Kate didn't let her gaze linger lovingly on the way the thin material hugged Ashley's full breasts.

"Look, Kate. We have to be careful. We have to cool it for a while."

"I thought we were being careful," Kate replied.

"We don't touch each other or anything like that when we're in public."

"It's not just that. We're always together, and people will, people have started to notice." Ashley brushed her hair back from her face.

"Don't you want to be together?" Kate asked, fighting to keep the tears out of her voice.

Ashley took Kate's hand. "You know I do. I love you, Kate. But I don't want people labeling us, either of us, and neither do you."

"You mean calling us lesbians?" Kate said softly, and Ashley looked away again.

"Among other things."

"If loving you means that's what I am, then I don't mind being called a lesbian," Kate said valiantly.

Ashley made a soft exclamation of disbelief. "You would if people knew."

"No, I wouldn't." Kate swallowed the lump in her throat. "Are you trying to say you don't want us to be together any more?"

"No," Ashley said fiercely and pulled Kate to her, wrapping her arms around her almost desperately. "I don't want that. I mean" — Ashley drew back to look at Kate — "I mean, we have to be sensible. We need to go out with guys occasionally, as camouflage if you like, so no one will suspect anything."

Kate turned away. "I don't want to go out with anyone but you."

Ashley firmly pulled Kate back into her arms. "Oh, Kate. Don't you see? We have to."

"Someone's said something, haven't they?" Kate asked.

"No," Ashley denied quickly, her face flushing guiltily.

"Yes, they have," Kate stated.

Ashley sighed. "It was Tim," she said softly and Kate felt a wave of fear. "You know how Dean plays football with Baden and Tim and that he's a good friend of theirs? Well, Dean must have said that I'd refused to go out with him or something, and Tim asked me what was wrong with Dean and why wouldn't I go out with him. One thing led to another, and we had a huge argument over it. Then he said we should watch out because people would think we, you and I, were, well, dykes."

Kate felt numb. What would have even put such an idea into Tim's head?

"So I said I'd go out with Dean to the movies tomorrow night," Ashley finished. "It's no big deal, Kate. And it'll keep Tim quiet."

"Oh, Ash. Why do we have to do all this pretending?" Kate appealed.

Ashley shrugged. "We won't always have to. Just until we're old enough to, you know, be together."

"We're seventeen," Kate bit out rebelliously. "That's old enough."

"Kate, please," Ashley entreated. "Bear with me on this. I don't want to start anything with Mum and Dad. Otherwise they might make it difficult for us to go down to university in Brisbane together."

Kate considered that aspect and reluctantly acknowledged Ashley might be right. She sighed dejectedly. "I hate all this subterfuge."

"So do I. Look, Kate, why don't you go to the

movies with Phillip? He's always asking you to. We could make a foursome."

"I don't like Phillip Walker." And apart from that, Kate didn't think she could watch Ashley and Dean together.

"And I'm not that keen on Dean Andrews either, but at least we could sit together. And going to the movies with them doesn't mean we have to marry them. Kate, can't you see? It'll make us look, well —"

"Normal?" Kate put in bitterly.

"Well, yes." Ashley sighed. "Kate, if Mum and Dad found out about us they'd really flip. Remember that sermon at church last weekend?" Ashley bit her lip. "I felt as though Pastor Jones was speaking directly to us. It was awful."

"I'm sure he's mistaken. I can't see a God who preaches love making us the way we are if it's so wrong."

"Maybe we're supposed to deny it, Kate. Like all the other sins."

"It's not a sin. We love each other, Ash." Kate put her arms around Ashley and felt the other girl's body stiffen. "How can that be wrong?"

Slowly Ashley relaxed and leaned into Kate. "In my rational moments I can see that, but sometimes I just get scared about it all. I don't think I could take it if everyone knew. Can you imagine how much they'd tease us, especially the guys. It would be horrible."

"Teasing can only hurt you if you let it," Kate said a little self-righteously. "You know I found that out. In fact you were the one who told me that."

Ashley raised her eyebrows, and Kate shrugged.

"Remember when I first came here? The

bushranging Ballantynes. The other kids used to tease me about my great-uncles being bushrangers who held up the gold coaches. If you don't react, they soon get sick of it." Even as she said it, Kate realized it wasn't quite as easy as that. But they were older now.

"Do you want to be talked about like Maggie and Georgie?" Ashley asked quietly.

Kate knew who Ashley meant. Maggie owned the local drapery store. She wore floral dresses and makeup. While Georgie, a mannish-looking woman, worked as a golf pro at the local club. Both in their late fifties, the women lived together and that they were lesbians Kate had little doubt. But she told herself there were no similarities between Maggie and Georgie and herself and Ashley.

"All those crude jokes and snide remarks behind their backs," Ashley was saying.

"We aren't like Maggie and Georgie," Kate said without much conviction.

"Aren't we?" Ashley sighed. "I've always felt sorry for them and wanted to, you know, talk to them, ask them about, well, it."

"Most people seem to like and accept Maggie and Georgie." Kate pulled on her T-shirt and shorts.

"Yes, but when push comes to shove they laugh at the jokes made about them," Ashley stated with embittered conviction.

"All I know is that I love you, Ash," Kate repeated earnestly. Ashley nodded.

"I know. And I love you too. But we have to be sensible. Don't you see that, Kate?"

"I guess so," Kate conceded reluctantly.

"Then you'll go to the movies with Phillip? As I said, we can make sure we still sit together."

"It won't be the same." Kate tried to hold out against Ashley's rationale.

"It'll be better than not being together at all."

"Phillip hasn't asked me."

"Don't worry about that. I'll mention it to Dean when he rings tonight. He can give Phillip a shove in that direction."

"What if Dean doesn't want Phillip and me along?"

Ashley laughed. "He will. I'm sure there won't be any problems there. Dean's pretty smitten with me."

"He's not the only one," Kate said dryly as she fought to quell a surge of pure jealousy. "And it's only for tomorrow night, isn't it? I mean, we don't have to do this every weekend, do we?"

"No. Of course not," Ashley reassured her.

But it had rather set the scene, Kate remembered with that same acute pain. She'd come to wish fervently that Dean would have to be on duty at the hospital every weekend.

And how she'd hated sitting there, so close to Ashley but unable to touch her, while Dean Andrews slipped his arm around Ashley's shoulders in a gesture of possession.

Kate recalled one night when she'd gone to the rest room with Ashley at intermission. On the way back Ashley had stopped to talk to one of her aunts.

"See you back inside, Kate," Ashley had said. "Tell Dean I won't be long."

Kate returned to her seat, feeling miserable at Ashley's offhandedness, even though she knew it was all just for show in front of her aunt.

"Where's Ashley?" Dean asked, looking toward the back of the theater.

"Talking to her aunt. She won't be long." Kate felt

herself stiffen as Dean moved over into Ashley's seat beside Kate.

She took a sip of her drink, eyeing Dean out of the corner of her eye. She had to grudgingly admit he was good looking in a dark, pretty-boy sort of way. He was older than Tim Maclean, more Ashley's brother Baden's age, and far too old for Ashley, Kate thought. He was smart and was in his first year of residency at the local hospital. Tall and well built, he had thick dark hair and a square-jawed, angular face. Every girl's dream, she reflected sarcastically to herself. But not hers. And hopefully, not Ashley's.

"While Ashley is away I want to ask you something," Dean was saying, and Kate turned to him in surprise.

"What?"

"You're her best friend. Has she mentioned anything to you about what she wants for her birthday?"

"Her birthday's not for ages," Kate said, and he nodded.

"I know but I want to get her something special."

"I don't know." Kate was noncommittal, and she barely registered the fact that Phillip had rejoined them.

"Get her an engagement ring and be done with it," Phillip said, and Kate was shocked into silence.

Dean frowned. "I've been thinking about that. In fact, I sort of mentioned it to her father last week, but he thinks Ashley might be a little young. You know, to get married."

"Ashley wants to go to university," Kate said desperately, and Dean smiled.

"She won't have to do that. I can afford to keep her. I've nearly finished my residency, and then I'll be going back south. We can live in a unit my parents own back in Melbourne. I've thought it all out."

Kate was horrified. She wanted to ask him if he'd talked to Ashley about this, but Ashley returned at that moment and Dean moved back to his own seat. As Ashley sat down, Kate felt the familiar warmth of Ashley's arm so close to hers, and she felt sick with dread. Things had become progressively worse after that night, culminating in the argument Kate and Ashley had had over Ashley going to the football club dance with Dean.

The murmur of voices, voices closer than the sounds that emanated from the Maclean backyard, brought Kate back to the present. And when Ashley looked over the side of the tree-house floor, for one moment Kate thought she was dreaming. Ashley smiled, but there was a certain wariness in her eyes.

"Hello, Kate. I didn't realize you were here. Jenny and I were just going to show Josh the tree house," she said brightly. "Do you mind? Or are we intruding?"

"Mum said I couldn't come over without her," Jenny beamed at Kate as she clambered up beside her mother. "But I said you said you didn't mind. You don't, do you?" Jenny persisted as Kate made no comment.

"I . . . no, of course not. As long as you're careful climbing up," Kate said, and Jenny swung herself up beside Kate.

The young girl turned. "Come on, Mum. Josh can't get up if you keep blocking his way."

There was a flurry of arms and legs, and then the tree house seemed full of people. Kate stayed in her chair, mainly because she suspected her rubbery legs would give way if she tried to stand. All she could recall was the feel of Ashley's body pressed so close to hers the afternoon before. And her heartbeats set up an erotic tattoo.

Ashley subsided onto the fruit crate, and Jenny organized her young cousin to sit beside her on the floor.

"Remember Josh, Kate? Aunt Belinda's son? You met him in the library." Jenny smiled Ashley's smile and turned to the boy. "Kate's Mum's best friend," she said seriously.

Josh Harrison murmured a shy hello to Kate, and she fancied she could see a ghost of a resemblance to Ashley in the young boy's features, a legacy of his mother, Belinda.

"Mum was telling Josh how she found you here the first time and how you became best friends from that day onward," Jenny said wistfully. "I wish I had a best friend like that."

Kate shot a quick glance at Ashley and saw a light flush color her cheeks.

"You've got lots of friends, Jen," Ashley said gently, and the child pursed her lips.

"But not special friends like Kate, friends you have exciting adventures with."

"We could have plenty of adventures in this tree house. It's cool," Josh put in. "It could be Duke

Nukem's base while he saves the world," he added eagerly, and Jenny, distracted, turned to him, her eyes glowing.

"Or a pirate ship, and we could sail the seven seas in search of gold doubloons and pieces of eight."

"It was a magic carpet for Kate and me," Ashley said with a smile. "We rode it to every corner of the world. Remember when we decided it was a Cobb and Co. coach and we were taking the gold from the diggings to the bank?"

Kate made herself smile. "Yes. I remember."

At her tone Ashley's smile faltered a little, but the two children didn't notice as Jenny was showing Josh how they could see into their grandparents' backyard.

"Gran's just arrived home," Jenny announced, and Ashley sighed.

"You two better head home then. Gran will be worried if she doesn't know where we are."

"Oh, Mum." Jenny grumbled. "But we just came over."

"You can come over again another day."

"Aren't you coming home, too?" Jenny asked as she followed Josh off the platform.

"In a minute. I want to talk to Kate for a moment. Tell your grandmother I won't be long."

Jenny looked as though she was going to argue with her mother, but she sighed loudly, said good-bye to Kate, and disappeared from view.

Ashley peered through the leaves, watching until the two children had slipped through the fence, and then she turned back to Kate.

"Kate. We should talk," she said softly, and Kate's already taut body tensed even more. "About yesterday afternoon."

"Forget it, Ashley. It was just" — Kate swallowed — "a mistake," she finished unevenly.

"A mistake?" Ashley repeated and gave a soft, humorless laugh. "I don't think it was, Kate. And neither do you. Mistakes don't leave you breathless and feeling as if you'll die if you don't get to repeat that kiss again."

"Ash, don't."

"Kate, please. I need to talk to you." Ashley sat down on the packing case, rested her elbows on her knees, and clutched her hands together in front of her. "This is tearing me apart."

"That's how I felt when you married Dean Andrews." Kate regretted the words even as she said them, and she felt a stab of pain as Ashley blanched.

"Don't you think it hurt me too? God, Kate. I loved you."

"I find that hard to believe," Kate said caustically.

"Why do you think I came back?" Ashley asked.

Kate shrugged. "It's your mother's birthday."

"For heaven's sake, Kate. What's made you so hard? You never used to be like this."

"It's not being hard. It's called self-preservation," Kate said rationally, and Ashley shook her head.

"Do you know that sometimes it was only the thought of you that kept me sane," she said quietly.

Kate told herself not to allow her aching heart to clutch at the other woman's words. She had to remain aloof, not let Ashley weaken her hard-won resolve.

"I cried all through my wedding." Ashley grimaced. "Everyone thought they were tears of happiness. Can you believe that? Happiness? I felt as though my life was over, and in a way it was."

"That's ridiculous," Kate protested.

"It's true, Kate. These ten years have become a blur of pretense, of hiding the real me deep inside myself and not letting me out. Because I was afraid of what I'd do. If it hadn't been for Jenny, I don't think I'd have made it."

Kate swallowed. "If it was so bad, why did you stay with him?"

"I tried to leave him dozens of times. But our families, either his parents or mine, always banded together, convinced me I had to go back, make a go of it for Jenny's sake. And each time I went back, Dean was more malicious in his paybacks."

"He physically abused you?" Kate asked hollowly.

"Only in the beginning. But after I came home the first time, before Jen was born, I told my parents, and Dad talked to him. I don't know what he said, but Dean never hit me again. But he found other, just as hurtful, just as belittling ways of getting back at me if I didn't go along with what he wanted, what he said."

A sudden shaft of anger aimed at Dean Andrews sliced through Kate, and she had to look away, not wanting Ashley to see that her words had slithered under Kate's guard. "So why are you divorcing him now?" she asked levelly.

"Dean thought he had the trump card. Our daughter. And our parents played on that, too. I was chock-full of guilt when I thought about breaking up the family and taking Jen away from Dean. I mean, you read all the books that say bad parents are better than no parents, etc.

"And then, one day when Dean had left the house after one of his tirades, Jen asked me why I didn't divorce her father when it was obvious I was happier when I wasn't with him? Just like that." Ashley snapped her fingers.

"I realized how inadvertently selfish I'd been, totally involved in how much I wanted to get away from Dean. I hadn't been watching Jen, asking her how she felt. It was then I saw that she was a different child when Dean was in the house. She was quiet and withdrawn, and she watched her father constantly to gauge his reactions. There was always a continuous tension around both of us. When Dean left she relaxed, just like I did.

"That was over two years ago. That's when I decided to make some changes in our lives. I'd been playing around with writing *Gold Fever* for ages, so I began to take it seriously. When I finished it, I rang a well-known agent and convinced her to read it. And it went from there. Having the book do so well has opened up other opportunities for me, so I can now afford to provide for us. I just regret I didn't do it sooner.

"When I stood up to Dean, he backed down. Of course, the fact that he had a mistress may have had something to do with it."

"I'm sorry," Kate said inadequately and a heavy silence seemed to stir the air in the fine leaves of the tamarind tree above them.

They sat in the uneasy silence, each lost in her own troubled thoughts.

"I won't believe you didn't think of me over the years." Ashley's voice was low, and it flowed sensuously over Kate's hot body like warm oil.

Kate met Ashley's gaze and was unable to look away, suddenly so sure she could drown in their inky blue depths. She was being drawn in, getting caught in the vortex of emotion that swirled about them both.

Ashley reached out, took Kate's hand in hers, lifted it to her lips. And Kate's senses leaped at the scorching touch, the fire of desire threatening to engulf her.

"Didn't you sometimes think of me, Kate?" Ashley repeated, her voice almost a whisper, lowly inciting, and Kate snatched her hand away.

"Did I think of you?" Her lips twisted into a humorless smile. "Oh, yes, I thought of you."

CHAPTER NINE

"In the beginning I thought about you almost constantly," she continued flatly, memories of the past rising, causing well-remembered pain. "I was slowly falling to pieces, not eating, closeting myself in my room, and I was failing my courses.

"Finally someone, a friend, convinced me I had to do something about it. So I made a pact with myself. I started out only allowing myself to think of you six times a day. And then I cut it back to four. Then sometimes I wouldn't even think about you for a week.

"I was so good at it." Kate gave a soft, self-deprecating laugh. "And then someone would walk along the street in front of me, someone with long golden hair that swung in the breeze just the way yours did when it was longer." Kate's gaze went to the soft tendrils of Ashley's now short hair, and she reached out, picked up one strand, let it slide through her fingers. "Or I'd get a faint scent of some perfume that you used to wear. And then" — she shrugged — "it would start all over again."

"Oh, Kate." A tear spilled over and trickled down Ashley's pale cheek. "I'm sorry."

"That was in the beginning, Ash. I'm over that now. But it was agonizing, and that's why I don't want to go through it all again."

"I —"

"Mum!" Jennifer's young voice came from below, and Ashley hurriedly wiped her face on the sleeve of her blouse.

Kate stood up, her legs and arms stiff from the tension that held her. "We'd better go down," she said quietly.

Ashley looked at her for long moments, and then she nodded unhappily.

"We're coming, love," she called to her daughter, and Kate followed her as she climbed from branch to branch.

"Mum, Gran said to ask Kate if she'd like to come to the party tomorrow night," Jenny said importantly. "You will, won't you, Kate?"

Patsy Maclean wanted Kate to come to her birthday party? Kate couldn't believe it. And what was more to the point, Did she want to go? she asked herself.

"Oh, I don't know, Jen. I —"

"Ah, Kate. Please come," Jenny pleaded. "We're having stacks of excellent food, and everyone will be there. Oh, and Gran said to bring your boyfriend if you'd like." She looked up at Kate. "Do you have a boyfriend, Kate? Is he nice?"

Ashley's gaze held Kate's again, and then Kate shook her head.

"No, Jen, I don't have a boyfriend," she said evenly, and the little girl frowned.

"Gran said you did. She said he worked in the big city hall."

"I know who your grandmother means, but he's not my boyfriend." So Patsy Maclean still thought Kate was safely involved with Phillip Walker. Or hoped she was? Was that why she'd issued the invitation?

"Why don't you come, Kate," Ashley said as she brushed a wayward strand of fair hair back from her daughter's face. "I know Baden and Tim would be pleased to see you again."

"Maybe," Kate said without conviction, knowing she wouldn't go.

"Mum always says maybe when she means no," Jenny said with childlike insight, and Kate had to smile.

"I promise to consider it. How's that?"

"Not as good as a 'Yes, I'll come,'" Jenny said and clutched at Kate's hand. "It'll be fun, Kate. You'll see."

Kate shot a quick glance at Ashley. "I'm sure it will be," she said, more than a little disconcerted.

* * * * *

So Kate had spent the last twenty-four hours wavering between going to the party and not going to the party. Now, late the next afternoon, she found herself dressing for Patsy Maclean's birthday celebrations with far more than her usual care.

And she still kept asking herself why she'd decided to go. *Because Ashley would be there*, an inner voice jeered, and she tried to push the disturbing thought from her mind, not wanting to face the truth of that implication.

Dress was casual, Ashley had said when she phoned a couple of hours ago, and her call hadn't helped Kate's indecision.

Ashley had been dispatched to the supermarket for some last-minute party fare, and she'd made her call from a pay phone there. Away from listening ears, she'd explained.

"I was just calling to see if you're coming this evening," she'd said, and Kate's hand had tightened on the receiver.

"I don't think it would be in everyone's best interests, do you?"

"It was Mum's idea," Ashley reminded her, and Kate pulled a mocking face at herself in the mirror over her dressing table.

"Only if I was coming with Phillip Walker," she put in. There was a moment's silence when all Kate heard was the faint sound of Ashley breathing.

"I wish you'd come, Kate," she said softly.

"And spend the whole night making sure I wasn't talking to you every time your mother appeared?"

"Does that mean you'd want to be talking to me?" Ashley asked lightly and gave a loud sigh. "No one but Mum knows what happened with us, Kate. But apart from that, what does it matter what anyone thinks? We're hardly children any more."

"You've certainly changed your tune," Kate said dryly. "I seem to remember that what everyone thought ranked rather high on your list."

"That was years ago, Kate. And please don't make me keep apologizing for it. I admit it was wrong, but that's easy to say with hindsight."

Kate sighed. She knew Ashley was right. But didn't she have grounds for continuing to labor the point? Or was she becoming shrewish?

"I'd really like you to come tonight," Ashley was saying. "And there're no strings attached. I won't even try to talk to you if you don't want me to."

"That might look a little strange, don't you think?"

"Okay. That gives me permission to talk to you," Ashley said gleefully. "And I promise to keep my hands to myself."

Kate's pulses leaped as her mind cast before her a picture of Ashley's hands on Kate's naked body. "Don't, Ash."

" 'Don't keep my hands to myself,' or 'Don't! Keep your hands to yourself!'?"

"You know what I meant. This isn't a game, Ashley." Part of Kate wondered where she'd lost her sense of humor over the years. Ashley had always been able to make her laugh.

"I know it's not a game, Kate," Ashley said quietly. "It's much, much more than that. I guess we should change the subject. So, are you going to come tonight? Dress is casual."

Kate sighed. "I'll see how things go. I may just drop in for an hour or so. But I'm not promising," she added, backing away from a half-made decision.

"What was it Jen said about maybes?" Ashley asked ironically, and Kate heard her sigh again. "All right, Kate. I guess I'd better get back with this stuff or else they might send out a search party for me." She paused. "But I hope I see you tonight, Kate. Bye."

And the phone had buzzed in Kate's ear for long moments before she replaced the receiver in its cradle.

So now here she was trying to decide what to wear to Ashley's mother's birthday party and wondering why she was even considering going.

In the end she grew impatient with herself and pulled on her first choice, a pair of tailored bottle-green shorts and a paler green top. The shirt had a loose collar and no sleeves so it would be cool enough in the dry inland heat. At this time of year even at night the heat barely dissipated.

Kate tucked in her shirt and threaded a dressy leather belt through the waist loops of her shorts. She slipped on a pair of casual, flat-heeled shoes and looked at herself in the mirror behind her bedroom door.

She grimaced. What was that saying of her aunt's? Something about not being an oil painting? She certainly wasn't that, that was for sure. Kate remembered overhearing one of her teachers describing her as a plain little thing. And that, as Kate saw it, about summed her up.

She couldn't help grinning wryly as she asked herself why she bothered to even look at herself. No matter what she'd always see herself as a shade too tall, a little too thin and far too ordinary.

That should do wonders for her self-esteem, she thought as she turned to brush her dark hair.

In the kitchen she took a bottle of light white wine

from the refrigerator and slipped the bottle into a handheld cooler. On the counter was the brightly wrapped gift she'd bought Ashley's mother, a fine, English bone-china cup, saucer, and plate to go with her collection.

Well, she was ready. Her heartbeats seemed to jump, and she took a deep breath. Before she could change her mind, she resolutely locked the kitchen door and headed toward the back fence, reassuring herself that she was only going next door and that she could always come home if it all got too much for her.

Strangely, the Macleans' back garden was empty, although Kate could hear voices coming from the house. Only as she skirted the swimming pool did she notice the stocky man bending over the brick barbecue by the other fence.

He looked up in surprise at her approach.

"Stone the crows! Is that you, Katie Ballantyne?" Ashley's father, the only person to ever call her Katie, enveloped Kate in a bear hug, lifting her off her feet.

He stepped back to look at her, hands still on her shoulders. Bill Maclean wasn't a tall man, but he was broad and muscular, and Kate was pretty much on eye level with him.

"Were you always that tall or have I shrunk?" he asked with a twinkle in blue eyes his daughter had inherited.

"I think I grew." Kate laughed easily. She'd always got on well with Ashley's father. "I thought you mightn't recognize me."

"Not recognize you? I'd know your bones in soup. Now, let me look at you. Still as beautiful as you always were."

Kate gave a skeptical laugh, and he frowned.

"Well, you are. And I can't believe I'm the only one who's told you so." He shoved another piece of wood into the fire beneath the barbecue plate, brushing his hands together as he turned back to Kate. "Why haven't we seen you for so long?"

Kate swallowed nervously. "Well, I was working down in Brisbane for years and only came back when Aunt Jane became ill."

Bill Maclean tut-tutted. "Yes, I heard about her fall. And Jane Ballantyne was a stubborn old girl. Couldn't suffer help from anyone." He shook his head. "It's a bad business this getting old, Katie. It's hard enough to admit to yourself you aren't the person you used to be without having to tell the world." He chuckled. "Now isn't this a wonderful subject for a birthday bash? I'll have us all crying in our beer if I'm not careful."

"How about crying in our wine?" Kate lightly indicated her cooler, and they laughed together.

"Just name your poison. Anyway, come on in and reacquaint yourself with the family." He slung an arm around Kate's shoulder and headed them toward the open sliding glass door.

"All the kids are home this time. We've got beds set up everywhere," he continued. "Place looks like a br —" He stopped, revised his description. "We're pretty crowded, but Patsy's as happy as a pig in mud. She just dotes on the grandkids. We've got four, you know, and another due any minute. That's Tim's first. Belinda's got three, and Ashley's got one. Baden and his wife are dragging their heels in that department. Both say they're too busy to start a family." He turned to Kate. "You have any kids, Katie?"

"Oh, no," Kate said quickly, and he lifted her left hand, shaking his head at her ringless fingers.

"Not married either? What's wrong with the guys in the village these days?"

A giggle escaped Kate, despite herself. "Maybe I run too fast for them."

Bill Maclean roared with laughter, and he was still laughing when they entered the house.

The sliding glass door led into a huge rumpus room that ran the length of the back of the house. Tonight it was decorated with streamers and balloons and a bright HAPPY BIRTHDAY banner. The room seemed to be filled with people, and Kate felt a renewed stab of apprehension.

Then she met the guarded gaze of Patsy Maclean as she came toward them.

"Hello, Kate," she said lightly enough.

"Happy sixtieth birthday," Kate said quickly and handed her the gift she'd brought along.

"Thank you. I certainly don't feel sixty." She put Kate's gift carefully on the table with a mound of others. "I'm going to open all my presents after supper, but I must say they all look too nice to disturb."

"Yes, they do," Kate said inanely, suddenly wanting to run for the sanctuary of home.

"So, are you going to share the joke with us?" Patsy turned to her husband, and he slipped his arm around her waist and gave her an affectionate squeeze. "You and Kate were having a good old laugh when you came inside."

"Katie was just telling me she isn't married, and I was remarking on how slow young men are these days. I didn't let the grass grow under my feet when I met you, did I, love? I had you at the altar like greased lightning." He kissed her noisily on the cheek, and Patsy patted him affectionately.

"We all know who had whom at the altar before he could change his mind." She laughed. "You always told me marrying you was the best day's work I ever did."

"Did I say that?" Bill asked exaggeratedly.

"Yes, Dad, you did. More than once. I'm a witness." Belinda Harrison had joined them. She turned to Kate. "Hello, Kate. Good to see you again. Do you remember Patrick? You were at our wedding many many moons ago."

Kate laughed. "Yes, of course. Hello, Patrick." She shook hands with Belinda's husband.

Patrick Harrison was still a pleasant looking man with reddish hair that was turning gray. His face suddenly broke into a smile.

"Kate. Of course. Now I've got it. You're Ashley's friend."

In her peripheral vision, Kate saw Patsy Maclean stiffen slightly, and her husband gave her a puzzled glance.

"Ashley and I went to school together," Kate put in as evenly as she could. "But we haven't seen each other for years."

"Is that right? Well, Ash's here somewhere." Patrick looked around. "I'll go and find her."

I wish you wouldn't, Kate wanted to cry out, but she stood impotently as Patrick disappeared into the crowd of people.

"And I'd better go back and check the barbecue,"

said Bill Maclean. "Should be ready to start cooking. Want to come give it your eagle eye, Pats?"

Patsy Maclean excused herself and followed her husband outside.

"Can I get you a drink, Kate?" Belinda asked, and Kate held up her cooler.

"I have some white wine."

"You didn't have to bring that. We have plenty. Here, let me take it." She took the cooler from Kate. "I'll put it beside the fridge in the kitchen, and you can take it home with you. No point opening it when we've got grog pouring out our ears. I think Dad thought the whole city was coming tonight. One white wine coming up. I won't be long."

Kate looked around only to find that Ashley's mother had stepped back inside and they were standing on their own, face to face. There was an awkward silence, and Patsy fingered the strand of pearls at her throat.

"Thank you for asking me to the party," Kate said stiltedly. "The" — she swallowed — "the decorations look wonderful."

"Yes. The children had fun putting them up this afternoon." Patsy Maclean seemed as nervous as Kate was. "You came alone? I thought perhaps you might have brought Phillip Walker along with you."

"No. I came on my own." Kate paused, trying to decide what course to take with Ashley's mother. Taking a deep breath she chose to be honest. "Phillip and I are acquaintances. We just work together."

"Oh. I see. I thought someone said you were seeing each other."

"No, we're not."

"Oh," Patsy repeated, and that same strained silence fell again.

Patsy's eyes met Kate's, and they both looked hurriedly away. The past came tumbling vividly back, and Kate flushed at the memory of lying naked beside Ashley and looking up to see Patsy Maclean in the doorway of Ashley's bedroom, her face pale with horror.

Kate drew a steadying breath. She had to say something. And she didn't want Ashley's mother thinking she was — Was what? she asked herself. Heterosexual? Kate almost laughed.

"Phillip's in the middle of a divorce, and apart from that" — Kate made herself smile — "he was a crushing bore when we were teenagers, and he hasn't improved over the years, I'm afraid."

Patsy sighed. "Yes. Well, I knew his late mother, and she was a bit like that, too."

And suddenly they were both smiling.

"Maybe it's genetic," Patsy added, and they laughed together.

Kate turned slightly to glance around her, and the first person she saw was Ashley.

"Found her," Patrick said affably. "Can't believe you two were just kids at my wedding."

Ashley gave him a playful shove. "Hardly kids, Pat. We must have been about fifteen, so no doubt we were convinced we were incredibly grown up. I know I thought I was so cool in my mauve bridesmaid's dress. Remember that, Kate?"

Kate nodded. Ashley had looked beautiful. And after the wedding Ashley had kissed Kate for that first, unbelievably incredible time. She slid a quick glance at Ashley's mother. But apart from a nervous fingering of her necklace again, Patsy Maclean seemed at ease.

"One drink, Kate." Belinda appeared and handed Kate a glass of white wine. "Come and say hello to Baden's in-laws, Pat," she added and bore her husband off toward the other end of the room.

Ashley pulled a face. "Pat's the only one who can stand Baden's mother-in-law."

"Ashley," her mother admonished, and Ashley grinned.

"Come on, Mum. You know she even scares the daylights out of Dad."

Amazed at Ashley's composure, Kate fought the urge to down her wine in one gulp.

Patsy Maclean sighed. "Speaking of your father, I'd better take him some meat to cook. Otherwise he'll have the barbecue plate too hot and we'll end up with burned offerings again."

She made her way toward the kitchen, and Kate turned nervously back to Ashley.

Tonight Ashley wore a pair of short brushed denim overalls and a thin, pink cotton-knit shirt. She looked vivacious and incredibly beautiful, and Kate swallowed as an arrow of desire speared through her. She wanted to hold Ashley to her, feel the soft contours molding with her own. Did Ashley feel this same burning need? How Kate wished she knew what Ashley was thinking.

At that moment Ashley leaned toward Kate. "You look wonderful," she said thickly, and Kate's body grew hot with an almost irresistible craving.

She looked down at her wine glass, twisted the stem between her unsteady fingers. "Ash, don't. Not tonight. I don't think I could bear it."

147

Ashley's breath caught, and she looked into Kate's eyes with a sultry need that matched Kate's.

"Kate, I wish —" She drew in another steadying breath that thrust her breasts against the bib of her overalls, and Kate's knees nearly gave way beneath her.

Surely the other people around them must sense the scorching tension that seemed to smolder around them, to spark between the two of them.

"I think perhaps you're right. We'd better keep to mundane subjects." Ashley looked around her. "Let's go and sit down over there." She indicated the old sofa at the end of the room that was miraculously free, now that some of the guests had moved outside to talk to Ashley's father as he cooked the steaks and sausages.

Kate reluctantly followed Ashley and sank down onto the couch, putting a body's width between them. She took a quick sip of her wine, feeling its sharpness tickle her throat.

"So. Can we talk?" Ashley asked, and Kate shrugged. "I mean, it's pretty public, and we're sitting sedately apart. No one could possibly get the wrong idea."

"Ash!"

"I'm sorry," Ashley said quickly. She started to reach out to touch Kate but drew her hand back. "That was uncalled for, wasn't it? Can we start again?"

Kate nodded. "Perhaps we'd better."

"So what have you been doing these past ten years?" Ashley asked, and Kate gave her a dubious glance. "No. I mean it, Kate. I'm interested, and I really want to know."

"Well, I haven't done much really," Kate began. "I went down to Brisbane to university, got my degree, and then got a job."

"Like we planned to do," Ashley said softly, and Kate steeled herself against the wistfulness in her tone.

"Yes, like we'd planned," she said flatly.

"When I came home before Jen was born, I tried to contact you through the uni but, of course, they wouldn't give out any information. So why couldn't I find your name in the Brisbane phone book? Didn't you have a telephone?"

"I shared a private house with three other students. The house belonged to the parents of one of the guys, so the phone was listed in his name."

"One of the guys?" Ashley queried. "You shared with a guy?"

"A guy and a couple, and when they left two other female students moved in."

Ashley pulled at a frayed piece of cotton on the sofa cover. "I feel jealous of them all."

Kate went to speak, but Ashley looked up at her. "I know. I have no right." She sighed. "I wanted so much to be with you."

"I wanted that too," Kate admitted and swallowed the lump that lodged in her throat.

"Did you enjoy it? I mean, life at uni, being away from home, sharing the house."

"Yes to all three," Kate replied. "I found the courses at uni interesting, and as far as sharing the house, well, we all got on fairly well really. Rob and I — Rob's the guy whose parents owned the house — Rob and I still call each other a couple of times a year."

"Did you have a relationship with him?"

Kate rubbed at the dull ache between her eyes. "I presume you mean were we sleeping together? Why do you want to know? Would it change anything?"

"I guess that's another thing I've got no right to ask, isn't it?" Ashley was worrying the frayed sofa cover again.

"I guess it is."

They lapsed into a discomfiting silence.

"I suppose I'm just wondering if you'd, well, tried a guy?" Ashley said at last, and Kate flushed and shook her head.

"Ash!" she appealed.

"Did you?" Ashley persisted, and Kate sighed.

"No. No, I didn't. But everyone thought Rob and I were an item. It suited us both at the time. Rob was, is gay too."

"Oh."

"So does that satisfy your curiosity?" Kate asked flatly.

"I guess I was curious," Ashley conceded and then gave a quick laugh. "Not vicariously though. I just wondered about, well, if you'd liked it."

"Then I suppose my answer to that is, I don't know. I've never tried it."

What about you? The question danced about inside Kate, but she refused to give the query voice.

"Do you want to know if I enjoyed it?" Ashley asked, and Kate flushed guiltily, her expression giving her away.

"I don't think talking about this is going to achieve anything," Kate said half-heartedly, and Ashley grimaced.

"I suppose not. I mean, I'm such an expert on that subject." She gave that humorless laugh again. "It all left me pretty cold, actually. Which made Dean's accusations about my supposed infidelities quite ludicrous."

"He accused you of having affairs?" Kate couldn't stop herself from asking, and Ashley nodded.

"Especially when we were first married. But I'd be the first to admit that when it came to that side of our marriage Dean had a raw deal."

A small part of Kate momentarily delighted in this revelation, but she took herself to task. In all fairness she had no more right to feel that way than Ashley had to ask Kate questions about her sex life.

"I didn't . . . I mean, I could never relax. Eventually Dean sent me to a counselor. That did no good. After half a dozen visits, we all admitted defeat. And about four years ago we stopped doing it."

"Ash, maybe you shouldn't be —"

"Shouldn't be telling you this? Who else can I tell, Kate? Not Mum. She'd be embarrassed. I did confide some of it to Belinda, but she couldn't understand. She adores Patrick, and they're ecstatically happy."

Ashley sighed. "I'd hazard a guess that when Dean and I severed physical relations was when he began his affair with one of his nurses, I presume the one he's now living with. Not that I could really blame him. So I was a complete failure in bed as well as out of it."

"It takes two people to have a successful relationship," Kate said, feeling somehow inadequate when faced with Ashley's confidences. And when it came to relationships, Kate granted she could scarcely give advice. She hadn't exactly had any huge successes in that area of her life. She acknowledged that she'd treated Rosemary abominably.

"So I guess I'm not cut out to be a good-time girl," Ashley was saying with a bitter laugh. "But you and I, we had some good times." Her tone softened, reached out, threatened to enmesh Kate as a million treasured memories rose out of their pasts. "Didn't we, Kate?"

Kate couldn't have spoken if her life depended on it. Desire surged through her, enveloped her, and she wanted to pull Ashley to her again, feel her soft, smooth skin once more, the captivating contours of her body.

"I'm a pretty slow learner," Ashley continued. "But I guess I'm suffering from — how did you describe it, Kate? — from being stranded emotionally in adolescence."

Kate took another sip of her wine as she drew herself together. "I don't agree with that opinion."

"Neither do I, for what it's worth." Ashley shifted in the chair. The old springs creaked in protest, and Kate looked across at her. "All I know is that I love you," Ashley said, holding Kate's gaze.

The seconds ticked by, intoxicating and intensely taut. And as they did a whole array of emotions jostled inside Kate. Love and adoration. Anger and outrage. Betrayal and disloyalty. Apprehension and uneasiness. And a burning need to bury the past, scatter her reservations to the four winds, and take Ashley in her arms, on any terms, as long as they were together forever.

How long they sat there looking into each other's eyes Kate couldn't have told, but someone loudly calling Ashley's name dragged them both back to the present.

"Ashley. How're you doing?"

Ashley looked up and blinked in surprise. "For heaven's sake. Mickey?"

"Your cousin?" Kate followed her gaze, looking for their playmate from childhood. And then Kate stiffened, all thoughts of Ashley's cousin driven from her mind. There across the room was Rosemary Greig.

CHAPTER TEN

Kate swallowed. What was Rosemary doing here? Kate wasn't even aware that the other woman knew the Macleans.

"Remember Michelle?" Ashley was saying, smiling a welcome. "She's a couple of years younger than us."

"Oh, yes. Mickey." Kate tore her eyes from Rosemary's slim figure and noticed a young woman approaching them.

She had Ashley's coloring and build, and she wore faded jeans, fashionably torn at the knees, and a sleeveless leather vest that molded her full breasts.

The legs of her jeans were tucked into long leather boots, and as she lifted her head Kate noticed the light catch a diamond stud in her nose.

Kate's eyebrows rose. She hadn't seen Mickey since the other girl was about Jenny's age.

"Ash!" Mickey cried again and fell on Ashley, hugging her roughly.

People turned to look, smiling, and Ashley's mother, who happened to be passing, shook her head fondly and playfully slapped Mickey on the back.

"Don't you break my couch, Michelle Marie," she said, and Mickey straightened and laughed before subjecting her aunt to a similar bear hug.

"No doubt you remember your cousin Michelle, Ashley," Patsy said, still laughing. "She's home visiting her parents."

"Course she remembers me," Mickey said and bent down and kissed Ashley loudly on the cheek, displaying a generous expanse of cleavage as she did so.

"Wow! Aren't you something." Ashley laughed. "Talk about a head turner. Is this the same little girl who wore all those frilly dresses?"

Mickey clutched at her heart. "For which I will never forgive my dear mother."

Ashley turned to Kate. "You remember Kate, Mickey?"

"Sure do." Mickey turned and grinned at Kate, and to Kate's consternation she leaned across and planted a kiss on Kate's cheek.

Kate's eyes went to the rise of Mickey's breasts above the vest, and she flushed guiltily when Mickey caught her looking and winked outrageously at her.

"I don't know why you're deigning to talk to Kate

and me, Mick," Ashley was saying. "We used to do all sorts of things to dissuade you from playing with us."

"Yeah. Don't think I've forgotten. Like playing hide-and-seek with me, and when I hid you two didn't try to find me. And I thought I was being so clever. That was cruel," she said with a mock glower.

"I'm deeply ashamed," Ashley said, looking suitably chastened. "Will you forgive us?"

"We're being rude to your friend, Michelle," Patsy Maclean put in. "We've left her on her own."

"Oh, yeah." Mickey turned and beckoned behind her.

To Kate's dismay, Rosemary Greig joined them.

Mickey took Rosemary's hand for one possessive moment, a movement that Kate saw didn't go unnoticed by Ashley's mother. Was Mickey a lesbian? Surely not. Kate was astounded.

"Rosie," Mickey said easily. "Meet my Aunt Patsy, the birthday girl."

Rosemary shook hands with Ashley's mother and wished her a happy birthday. Then Patsy excused herself as Belinda called her from the patio.

"And this is my cousin, Ashley, and her friend Kate," Mickey continued the introductions.

Rosemary smiled. "Actually, Mickey, we've met."

"You have?" Mickey was surprised.

"At Kate's last weekend. I sort of work with Kate."

"When did you get home?" Ashley asked Mickey quickly as the other woman's eyes narrowed as she glanced from one to the other.

"About a week ago. I work in Sydney, and I just changed jobs. I have about five weeks before I start the new one, so I thought I'd come up and see the folks."

"Not married or anything?" Ashley asked, and Mickey threw back her head and laughed.

"Married? Not likely. I'm still enjoying the single life." She slid a knowing glance at Rosemary, and Kate stiffened.

There was no misinterpreting that look, Kate decided. Mickey must be gay. All the signs pointed to there being a relationship between her and Rosemary. But wouldn't Mickey be too flamboyant, too obvious for Rosemary's taste?

"Besides" — Mickey winked at Ashley — "I'm not your usual team player. I'm sort of way out in the left field."

Ashley raised her eyebrows, and Mickey lowered her voice. "I'm into women. I don't make a secret of it, but Mum and Dad prefer I don't shout it from the rooftops or swing from any chandeliers at these family dos."

"Oh. I see." Ashley glanced at Rosemary, and Mickey's grin broadened.

"I was lucky enough to run into Rosemary yesterday. We're old friends. We met in Sydney a couple of years ago before she moved to the Towers. I couldn't believe it when I saw her in the local café."

"Quite a coincidence," Rosemary remarked and looked at Kate. She gave a faint shrug, part apology and part defiance.

"Anyway, where's this daughter of yours, Ash?" Mickey looked around. "Mum says she looks just like you. What about taking me to meet her?"

Ashley's gaze went to Rosemary, and she hesitated, undecided.

"Rosemary can stay and talk to Kate," Mickey said, totally misconstruing Ashley's reticence.

"Jenny's probably out at the pool with Dad and the boys," she said at last, standing up. Her glance went from Kate to Rosemary. "We won't be long."

Rosemary immediately sat down beside Kate, taking the seat Ashley had vacated.

"I think she's a little jealous," Rosemary leaned forward and whispered to Kate.

Kate drew herself together, choosing to ignore Rosemary's remark. "I . . . it's a surprise to see you here, Rosemary," she said as evenly as she could, and Rosemary laughed softly.

"Me being here or me being here with Mickey?"

"Both, I guess."

Rosemary sobered. "Maybe I am outing myself to those who happen to be looking. Mickey's not exactly a closet dweller." Rosemary gave Kate a crooked smile. "You look a little stunned."

"I suppose I am. Apart from seeing you here, I'm still trying to bring ten-year-old Michelle up to Mickey today."

"She certainly is a character," Rosemary agreed. "But she's bright and fun to be with, too. She looks a little like Ashley, doesn't she?" She looked levelly at Kate. "So what about you and Ashley?"

Kate felt herself stiffen defensively, and Rosemary sighed and shook her head.

"Kate, don't let happiness slip through your fingers because of old angers and mistakes."

Kate went to speak, but Rosemary held up her hand.

"Hear me out, Kate. Stop and think about it. And forget about outdated social mores. I let that color my decisions, and it causes more grief than anything else. After the initial shock, what can happen? Some people will go on as they are now, and others might stop talking to you. The latter aren't worth worrying about."

"I wish it was that simple, Rosemary," Kate said with a sigh, and Rosemary patted her leg.

"It is that simple. Or it can be. You can make it so." She paused. "You still love her, don't you?"

Kate sighed again. "I don't know, Rosemary."

"As a casual, well, maybe not-so-casual observer, I'd say you both want each other desperately."

"That's ridiculous." Even as she said the words, Kate's foolish heart soared.

"I've seen the way you look at each other, Kate." Rosemary laughed. "And I know what I'm looking for. So, as I see it, you have two choices. One" — she marked the point off on her fingers — "make a go of it with her. Or two, at least have a raging affair with her and get it out of your system."

For some reason, Kate felt tears well up in her eyes. She looked away.

"No, perhaps the second point wouldn't work," Rosemary said gently. "I see she's in your blood, Kate, and maybe that only comes along once in a lifetime. You'd be a fool to let it pass you by."

"It was all such a mess, Rosemary," Kate said flatly. "And I'm terrified to take a chance again."

"I know. But consider the alternative."

Kate looked at Rosemary, and she smiled.

"It's a lonely life on your own, Kate."

"Hello. This looks like a so-serious conversation. Are you two trying to save the world?"

Kate and Rosemary looked up to see Tim Maclean standing in front of them. He crouched down and sat on the floor.

"Good to see you again, Kate," he said with a grin, and Kate gathered herself together enough to make the introductions.

"What a night, hey? It's beautiful having the whole family back together," he remarked after shaking Rosemary's hand.

Tim Maclean hadn't changed all that much, Kate decided, apart from a few flecks of gray in his hair at the temples.

Tim teased Kate with anecdotes from their childhood, and Kate began to laugh at his easy humor. Eventually when Tim started to talk about mutual childhood friends, Rosemary excused herself and went in search of Mickey. Tim took her place on the couch.

There was still no sign of Ashley returning, so Kate made herself focus on Tim. He made easy conversation, happy to fill her in on his branch of the family business in Townsville. He then told her at length of his approaching fatherhood and how thrilled he was to be starting a family at last. By the time Baden and his wife joined them, Kate knew all about scans and breathing exercises and other associated baby information.

By then the meal was served, and it was as delicious as any barbecue Kate had shared with the Macleans. Ashley was busy helping feed the large number of children present, but every so often her blue eyes would seek Kate out. She'd smile, and Kate's stomach would turn over as fire raced through her veins.

The birthday cake was brought out and Patsy Maclean blew out the candles before opening all her gifts and making a thank-you speech.

Not long after that, some of the guests with young

children started to leave. Jenny had come to sit with Kate, and Kate could see that her eyelids were drooping.

Ashley appeared and gently shook her daughter's shoulder. "Time for bed, Jen," she said, and the young girl frowned.

"Do I have to, Mum?"

"I think so. And remember we have to go to the station to see Gran and Granddad off on their trip in the morning."

Jenny pushed herself to her feet. "Did you know Gran and Granddad are going on a second honeymoon, Kate?"

Kate suppressed a grin. "No, I didn't."

"They're going down to Brisbane by train like they did when they got married. Then they're going to the beach for a week. And then they're flying down to catch the boat for their cruise. That's why Mum and I, oh, and Josh, are looking after their house."

Ashley shrugged at Kate. "Jen and I are house-sitting. Belinda and Pat and the two older boys are going home in the morning too. Josh is staying with us for the school break."

"Uncle Tim said he'd come down one day and take us gold panning," Jen said excitedly. "Where's Josh, Mum? I should go tell him."

"Josh went to bed half an hour ago. Now it's your turn, young lady. Say good night to Kate."

"'Night, Kate." And to Kate's surprise Jenny wrapped her arms around Kate's neck and gave her a hug. "See you tomorrow."

"Yes. Good night, Jen." Kate's eyes met Ashley's, and she suddenly wanted nothing more than to be part of this child's life. And her mother's.

161

The revelation shocked Kate to her very center. She'd never been interested in children, although she always enjoyed the storytelling sessions at the library. But to feel this enchantment with Ashley's daughter filled Kate with dismay, and she sat quietly trying to come to terms with the enormity of the idea.

Ashley went off to see her daughter settled in bed, and the rest of the guests began to leave. Kate supposed she should go home too, and she stood up, preparing to say good night to Patsy and Bill when they'd seen the last carload of guests drive away.

"It's been a great evening," she said to Belinda, and she groaned.

"Look at the time, though. Patrick went to bed an hour ago, the piker. This is way past my bedtime, let me tell you."

"You must be getting old, sis," Ashley teased, as she followed her parents into the room.

"We all are," said her sister dryly, and her mother laughed.

"Well, I'm going to take my old bones to bed," said Patsy Maclean, and her husband looked wounded.

"Calling me *bones* is bad enough, but I object to the *old* bit, love."

They all chuckled as Bill and Patsy said good night and left them.

"Well, I'll head off too," Kate said.

"Don't forget your cooler." Belinda hurried into the kitchen to collect it for Kate, leaving Kate momentarily alone with Ashley.

And suddenly Kate felt burning hot. Ashley's eyes played over her, and Kate felt as though she'd actually touched her. Her nerve endings tingled in anticipation, and she felt a dampness between her legs. She was totally attuned to Ashley, and if Belinda hadn't been with them . . .

As Belinda rejoined them and handed Kate her cooler, Ashley opened a cupboard and took out a flashlight.

"Could you check on Jen on your way to bed, Belinda? I'll just see Kate home." Ashley held up the flashlight. "Her back light's out."

"Okay." Belinda turned back to them. "Take your key, Ash, and Mum won't have to worry about you leaving the back door unlocked." She rolled her eyes at what was a family drill.

Ashley held up her keys, and Belinda laughed.

"There's no need for anyone to see me home," Kate told them. "It's quite moonlit out there."

"And there's no need to risk falling over something and breaking your ankle or anything," Ashley said firmly.

"Had that much wine, have you, Kate?" Belinda joked with Kate. "Just don't start entertaining the poor neighbors with dirty ditties like Baden used to." She laughed. "See you later. 'Night, Ash. I'll probably be asleep when you get back." She continued down the hallway.

"You don't have to do this," Kate repeated when they were alone.

"I know I don't. But I want to." Ashley stepped outside and waited for Kate to follow her. "You did the same for me the other evening."

And Kate vividly remembered what had happened that night in the shadows of the tamarind tree. And with the thought came that familiar burst of so seductive temptation.

Ashley turned and locked the door before slipping

163

the keys into her pocket. "Besides, I can use a bit of fresh air. Any more than two glasses of alcohol and I get a thick head. And I believe I've had more than two glasses. It feels like it, anyway."

They skirted the swimming pool, and Ashley slipped through the fence, switching on the flashlight so Kate could see.

"Remember that party we went to, can't remember whose it was, and I got sloshed? It was the one and only time I ever did that."

"It was at Mike Dunstan's," Kate said, remembering it well. She'd been really worried about Ashley. Dean had been working that weekend, and it was just after Ashley had been to the football club dance with him. Ashley had been so uncharacteristically reckless.

"Mike Dunstan's. That's right." Ashley laughed softly. "God, I was sick. But it cured me. I never drank too much again. Lucky you were there to get me home safely."

"And to get Belinda to help me sneak you into the house so your mother didn't see you."

"Believe me, Belinda never let me forget that. She was a real pain back then. Funny how sisters improve with age. Brothers too, I guess. Baden and Tim are quite bearable now. And who'd have thought Tim would be so dotty over the baby they're expecting."

"Tim told me they've waited a long time for this."

"They sure have. They were told they probably wouldn't be able to have any children so it's been something of a miracle for them." Ashley laughed. "The baby will probably be placid like Gail, but I'm hoping it will be fractious so Tim will realize what he was like to live with. He was such a pain. Talk about tease! He was the bane of my life when I was ten."

Kate smiled reluctantly as they started up the back steps. "You had your disagreements with him, that's for sure."

"Disagreements? It was all-out war. I don't know how Mum put up with us. She must have wished she'd had four kids like you."

"That's debatable in the circumstances," Kate said dryly, and Ashley stopped, one step up from Kate.

"She didn't really blame you, Kate," she said softly. "After you left she, we, had a long and wearing discussion about, well, crushes and growing up and what was considered normal." Ashley sighed and continued up the steps. "But that's history."

"I never meant to cause any dissension between you and your mother," Kate said unhappily.

"I know. And I suppose it was a wonder no one caught us before that. Looking back, we took a lot of chances."

Ashley held the flashlight on the door so Kate could insert her key. She stepped past Ashley and swung the door open, moving inside to feel for the light switch, flicking it on. She turned back to the door to see that Ashley had followed her inside.

The tension that wasn't far below the surface when they were together clutched at Kate again.

"Thanks for seeing me home," she said quickly, and Ashley shrugged.

"To tell you the truth I jumped at the chance to see you alone for a while."

Kate's mouth went dry, and she swallowed. "Well, it's late." She looked up at the old-fashioned kitchen clock that ticked loudly into the tense atmosphere. "It's after one a.m."

Ashley grimaced. "If we were going to turn into pumpkins, I think we'd already be squat and round and sort of orange colored."

They both laughed nervously.

And then they looked across at each other, and something shifted painfully in the region of Kate's heart. Someone made a soft, so low, moaning sound that drove everything from Kate's rational mind, leaving only Ashley, her beauty, and the wild, undampened attraction Kate still felt for her.

CHAPTER ELEVEN

And then they were in each other's arms. Kate couldn't have told who made the first move, but by the time Ashley's lips claimed hers she was way beyond caring. Ashley's tongue tip teased Kate's mouth, then slipped incitingly inside, inflaming Kate.

Kate gathered Ashley impossibly closer and felt the searing imprint of Ashley's entire body. Her full breasts nudging just below Kate's. Her hipbones hard against Kate's. They were thigh to thigh. And Kate's body burned to feel Ashley's naked warmth on hers.

"Oh, Kate, Kate," Ashley murmured brokenly, her

breath so erotically tantalizing against Kate's mouth that Kate trembled with inexpressible yearning.

Ashley slid her lips along Kate's jawline and teased at her sensitive earlobe. Kate's knees felt as though they'd gone to water. She leaned her hips back against the support of the countertop and closed her eyes, luxuriating in the sensuousness of Ashley's so soft lips on her supersensitive skin.

Ashley worked her way slowly back along Kate's jaw, skimmed alluringly over her chin, lingered to kiss Kate's trembling, craving mouth, slid down over the curve of her throat, paused at the throbbing pulse, its erratic beating the evidence of Kate's accelerating arousal.

Then Ashley's hand moved around to Kate's midriff, shifted upward to cup the small mound of Kate's breast. Her thumb gently teased Kate's hard nipple through her blouse, and Kate arched her back, tried to fumble with the buttons on her shirt.

"I want . . . I need you to touch me," Kate heard someone say and realized the voice was her own, thickly unrecognizable.

"Shh," Ashley whispered. "Let me." She dealt with the buttons and unbuckled Kate's belt, pulled the shirt from the waistband of Kate's shorts, and Kate heard Ashley's breath catch in her throat.

Kate wasn't wearing a bra, and Ashley pushed the material of Kate's blouse from her shoulders, her eyes on the bare breasts she'd exposed. And simply knowing that Ashley was looking at her, eyes languidly sensual, set goose bumps prickling all over Kate.

Ashley let out the breath she was holding and slowly bent forward, brushing one straining nipple with her tongue.

An eruption of pure desire exploded inside Kate, shock waves arrowing downward to set up an incessant, pulsating ache between her legs.

"Please, Ash —" She heard herself beg, and Ashley's lips returned to crush Kate's mouth, her hands cupping Kate's breasts, thumb and forefinger teasing Kate's nipples. Ashley's leg had insinuated itself between Kate's, abrading the throb that threatened to have her crying out, repeating Ashley's name like a litany.

Kate pushed aside the straps of Ashley's overalls and pulled at Ashley's T-shirt, freeing it from her pants. She slid her hands beneath the shirt, filled her trembling palms with the fullness of Ashley's lace-clad breasts.

Ashley moaned deep in her throat, and Kate released her, making Ashley move against her in protest, but Kate was only fumbling with the catch on Ashley's bra. It gave way, and she returned to caress Ashley's breasts that still molded the thin cotton of her T-shirt.

With trembling hands Ashley pulled her shirt upward and peeled the lacy bra away, freeing her breasts for Kate's eager touch.

For a long moment Kate let her gaze feast on their warm smoothness, before she reached out, hands reverently taking pleasure in their softness, their fullness. Then she lowered her mouth, sucking on one rosy nipple and then the other.

Kate let her tongue tip rasp over the swollen peaks and Ashley moaned again, leaning forward, and this time it was Ashley who clutched at Kate for support.

"God, Kate!" Ashley groaned. "I can't stand up much longer. I need to . . . we have to . . ."

Kate drew a steadying breath into her tortured lungs and nodded. She took Ashley's hand and led her along the hallway and into her bedroom. She flicked on the bedside lamp and pulled back the bedspread. A dull glow haloed the bed in a sphere of light, and Kate turned to Ashley, glancing a question at the lamp.

"Please. Leave the light on," Ashley whispered. "I need to see you. I want to watch you."

Kate's shirt was still on the kitchen floor, and she was naked from the waist up. Ashley moved forward and lightly reacquainted her hands with Kate's breasts until Kate's breathing quickened again. Then she unzipped Kate's shorts and knelt down to slide them and Kate's underpants from her hips. She paused, still kneeling in front of Kate, and she rubbed her soft cheek against the damp dark curls.

Kate's legs gave way then, and she sank down on the side of the bed. Ashley looked up at Kate, her eyes bright as sapphires in the dull light. She continued to hold Kate's gaze for a long moment before she stood up, peeled off her disheveled shirt, and discarded her bra.

Her breasts seemed to glow, opalescent in the yellowish tinge of the lamplight, the puckered nipples dark against her pale skin.

Kate drank in the supple sensuality of the other woman, and she felt a renewed dampness between her legs, pulsing her need.

As Kate watched, Ashley stepped out of her overalls and stood naked before Kate. Slowly Kate reached out, drew her forward, and buried her face between Ashley's breasts, inhaling the scent of her, drinking in the fragrance that was so totally Ashley.

Ashley pushed Kate gently backward and reached across her to slide a pillow beneath Kate's head, her breasts agonizingly close to Kate's own tingling breasts.

Then Ashley was straddling Kate, slowly leaning forward and over her, hovering but not quite touching her, and Kate's breath caught in intense expectation. When Kate thought she could barely endure the heightened anticipation, Ashley lowered herself until her breasts just brushed Kate's.

That so light touch set Kate's aroused senses clamoring, craving more, so very much more.

Kate gently took hold of Ashley's breasts, guided Ashley's hardened nipples to graze against her own. And then she moved her head, teasing Ashley's nipples with her tongue tip, and Ashley shivered, her breath stirring Kate's hair.

"That drives me insane," Ashley said thickly, and Kate slid one hand around over Ashley's hips, down over the swell of her stomach, until she could bury her fingers in Ashley's wetness.

She slid her fingers into the dampness, the musky scent of Ashley's arousal making Kate's blood rush through her veins. She let Ashley set the pace, move against her fingers, and then Ashley tensed, crying out Kate's name, her body settling over Kate's as her straining muscles relaxed.

Ashley took a ragged gulp of air, and then her lips found Kate's. "God, Kate, that was wonderful." She kissed Kate again, and then she was sliding down beside her, lips on Kate's breast, fingers teasing over Kate's flat stomach, slowly circling her navel, dipping enticingly into its indentation.

Kate arched her body, her nerve endings screaming

as every muscle in her body tensed, totally aroused, awaiting the caress of Ashley's fingers assuaging the hunger that throbbed between her legs.

"Please, Ash. Touch me," she entreated, and then Ashley's magic fingers were inside her, her lips caressing Kate's breast, and Kate exploded in wave after wave of orgasm.

Kate gradually drifted from her dreamless sleep. She seemed to float, euphoric, and she stretched languidly, feeling like a cat reclining in the sun. Her muscles protested slightly, bringing back the events of the evening before, and with that recall came a rush of conflicting emotions.

What have I done? jostled with *That was incredible.*

Kate's hands went to press on the sudden flutter in her stomach, and she realized she was completely naked beneath the bedclothes. She could remember Ashley pulling the white cotton sheet gently around her before she left.

After making love, they'd dozed in each other's arms, legs still entwined, skin slick with dampness from their exertions. Eventually Ashley had moved to kiss Kate's bare shoulder.

"I have to go," she'd said softly, and Kate turned her face toward her so that their lips met.

They kissed deeply, passion flickering to life again, and Ashley moaned, dragging her lips from Kate's.

"God, Kate! If we, if I stay any longer I won't have the strength to go."

"Then stay," Kate appealed, holding Ashley close.

"I wish I could, Kate. But if Jen wakes up and wonders where I am I, well ... It's best if I go back."

Of course Ashley couldn't stay. Even as she'd suggested it, Kate knew she couldn't.

"I'll — Will I see you tomorrow?" Ashley asked, and Kate nodded her head.

Ashley looked into Kate's eyes. "This has been" — she shook her head slightly — "what can I say? I love you, Kate. It cuts me up that I have to go when I so much want to stay with you now."

"I know."

Ashley gave her a quick kiss and slipped out of bed. She pulled on her discarded clothes and turned to kiss Kate's breasts before slowly pulling the sheet over Kate. She placed a lingering kiss on Kate's lips, and then she was gone.

Tingling with remembered awareness, Kate glanced lazily at the clock, only to sit bolt upright when she realized it was after ten-thirty. She'd had the longest night's sleep she'd had in months. She crossed to the en suite and slipped beneath a tepid shower, her hands straying to the places Ashley's hands had strayed the evening before.

She and Ashley had made love just like they'd used to do. Kate hesitated. No, it hadn't been like before. It was so much, much more than it had been before. Kate switched off the shower and began to towel herself dry.

She looked up and caught her reflection in the bathroom mirror. She looked different, fancied her features were softer somehow. Hastily she looked away, not wanting to admit how much last night had meant to her. Admitting such a thing meant she had to face the truth and make some decisions about it.

In something of a dazed state, Kate made herself some toast and tried to concentrate on reading the Sunday papers. An hour later she didn't recall eating the toast and had no idea about the contents of the newspapers.

Exasperatedly she cleared away her breakfast dishes and chose the chore she liked the least. Although her mind was far from on it, she spent the next few hours ironing and preparing her clothes for work next week.

Kate was standing in the middle of the kitchen in a fever of indecision. She desperately wanted to see Ashley, but she felt apprehensive. Yet she knew they had to talk.

She glanced at the kitchen clock. Surely Ashley would be on her own now. Kate was about to move toward the door when the sound of running feet pounded on the back steps. She was halfway across to the door when someone began knocking. Ashley stumbled into the kitchen as Kate swung the door open.

"Ashley —" Kate began, memories of the night before making her skin prickle and warm color heat her face. Then she realized Ashley's own face was pale with anxiety.

She grabbed Kate's arm urgently. "Kate, have you seen the kids?" she asked breathlessly, and Kate shook her head.

"No. Not since" — Kate swallowed — "not today. Why? What's wrong?"

"They're gone, and I can't find them anywhere. God, where could they be?" Her words began to run together, and Kate took her hand.

"Calm down, Ash. Calm down," Kate said soothingly. "How long has it been since you've seen them?"

"I don't know." Ashley threaded her fingers distractedly through her hair. "A couple of hours, I think."

"Did you check the tree house?"

"Yes. On my way over. I even went right up the ladder just in case, well, in case they just weren't answering." Ashley clutched at Kate, and Kate slipped her arms easily around her, gently rubbing her tense back.

"I was tired, after last night, and getting Mum and Dad to the railway station and seeing everyone off home. It was so hectic. After they'd all left I thought I'd have an hour's rest before coming over to see you. But I fell asleep.

"The kids were watching television. I lay down and picked up a magazine, and I must have dozed off. When I woke up two hours later they were gone. Oh, Kate, where can they be? It's not like Jen to go off without telling me like this, and I wouldn't have thought Josh would either."

"They didn't leave a note?"

Ashley shook her head. "No." She glanced at her watch. "God, Kate, they could have been gone for two hours or more. What will I do? Jenny's never done anything like this before."

"I'm sure they've just forgotten the time," Kate reassured her, and Ashley ran her hand over her eyes.

"It's already five o'clock, and Jen knows to be home by then, regardless. Something's happened to her, Kate. I just know it."

Kate pulled Ashley into her arms again. "Come on now. You don't know that. What about any of her friends you could ring?"

"She hasn't really made any friends here yet. There's just Josh. Oh, Kate . . ." Ashley buried her face in Kate's shoulder.

"Did you notice if their bicycles were missing?" Kate asked, and Ashley looked up quickly.

"No. Come on. Why didn't I think of that. I looked in the garage too." She headed back down the steps, and Kate followed her, Ashley running to the back fence, slipping through the gap.

"They've gone. Their bikes are gone," Ashley said shrilly. "I'll get in the car and go looking." She turned to Kate. "Will you come with me?"

"Of course. But let's just check the house again." Ashley followed Kate inside, and they both called out to the two children. But there was no reply, the house throwing back that empty, echoing silence. They closed the door and headed for Ashley's mother's car.

"Oh, God!" Ashley said in despair. "Where could they be?"

Kate tried to quell her own mounting fear. "Let's try the corner store. We'll go in and ask Jo if she's seen them. Maybe they went there for an ice cream or something. Want me to drive?"

Ashley nodded and handed Kate the keys. She backed the car out onto the road and drove around the corner, pulling up outside the small convenience store. Ashley raced in, only to return with the knowledge that the two children hadn't visited the shop.

For the next half hour or so they drove around the town, through the main street, by the park, but there was no sign of the children. They returned to check the house to no avail. By now Ashley was pale and silent and Kate felt at a loss as to what to do next.

"I think we should go to the police, Kate," Ashley said flatly, wrapping her arms around herself.

Kate nodded and headed back toward the car. "If they took their bikes they must have been planning on going some distance," Kate reasoned. "Would they have set out to ride to the weir or maybe to the river?"

"I don't know," Ashley replied brokenly, and tears ran down her cheeks. "I just can't believe Jen would go anywhere without asking me first. Someone must have taken them, Kate," she said flatly, her face ashen.

Kate put her arms around her again and held her close, her hand moving soothingly in Ashley's soft hair. "We don't know that."

Kate went over the few conversations she'd had with Jenny. When the young girl had visited the library for the storytelling session, they'd talked about the history of the town and the mines. Would she and Josh have gone exploring?

"Ash, you don't think they'd have — ?"

Ashley's sobs subsided, and she straightened, drawing herself together.

"Have what?" Ashley asked.

Kate bit her lip. "When Jen was in the library last week we talked about the gold mining days. She asked me about the mines, the ones still open, and then she said you'd told her stories about the old Eureka mine we used to play near when we were kids. I warned her it wasn't safe then or now. You don't think they would have gone exploring out there, do you?"

Kate watched Ashley's face tense as the same unspoken fears cross her mind. "It's worth a try," she said, and Kate started the car, spinning the tires as she pulled out onto the road again.

As Kate headed out toward the old mine site, bitumen gave way to gravel, and then the road became a track of two uneven, overgrown wheel ruts. Eventually they had to leave the car, and they both began to run toward the barbed wire fence that they knew posted warnings of private property and dangerous mine shafts.

Ashley stumbled, and as Kate grabbed her arm to steady her they saw the two bicycles propped against a stunted china apple tree.

"Oh, God! Kate, those are their bikes," Ashley said agitatedly and began to run toward the fence again.

Kate grabbed a strand of barbed wire with one hand and put her foot on the other, making an opening for Ashley to climb through. Then Ashley turned and did the same for Kate.

"Oh, Kate. Surely they wouldn't have gone into the mine. What if . . . ?"

At that moment they heard a sound, and they both turned to see a distraught Josh running headlong down the slight hill toward them.

"Aunty Ash! Aunty Ash!" he cried and threw himself into her arms.

CHAPTER TWELVE

Ashley fell to her knees and tried to calm him.

His shirt was torn, and Kate drew a breath as she saw that his exposed shoulder was grazed and dark with dried blood. Tears streaked through the dirt on his face, and he drew gulping sobs. "It's Jen. She can't get out. I couldn't shift the wood."

Kate unobtrusively examined his arm and satisfied herself the wound had stopped bleeding. "Show us where," she said as they turned him back toward the mullocky hill where the old, boarded-up mine shaft was.

"We just went in a little way to see what it was like," Josh told them as they hurried through the tinder, dry spear grass, none of them noticing the spiky barbs that clutched at their bare legs and shorts. They followed the overgrown track through spindly trees and clumps of dark green rubber vines.

"We moved some of the wood until we could squeeze inside and it was dark and then some wood fell on us." Josh gulped again. "I didn't want to leave her, but Jen said you'd be looking for us now because we said in the note we'd be home at five. When it got later, Jen said I had to come and get you." He started to cry again as they came up to the timber-covered mine entrance in the side of the hill.

"I know we shouldn't have gone in," Josh said and started to lead the way into the mine.

"Just a minute, Josh." Kate took hold of his arm. "Let us check it out first." She examined the timber and carefully pulled a couple more pieces aside to make a bigger opening. "One of us had better stay outside. What do you think?" she said, looking meaningfully at Ashley. "Shall I just go and have a look?"

"No, Kate." Ashley clutched Josh to her side for a moment. "I'll come in too."

Kate wanted to argue the point, but she also didn't want to upset Josh any more.

Ashley turned to the young boy. "You wait here by the opening. We may need you to run for help. Okay?"

Josh nodded miserably and wiped his eyes with his T-shirt, further smearing his face with dirt.

Slowly and cautiously Kate slipped into the dusty dark cavity of the mine, feeling Ashley close behind her. She stopped inside to allow her eyes to adjust to the dark.

"Jen?" Ashley's voice broke, and Kate heard her take a calming breath. "Kate and I are here," she said softly.

A beam of a flashlight flicked on, momentarily blinding Kate, and she held up her hand to shield her eyes.

"Mum. Kate. I'm over here," Jen said, unable to disguise her relief, and Kate's gaze followed the beam of light about ten feet in front of her and slightly to the right. "I was saving the batteries in case —"

"Shine the light on the ground so we can see to get to you."

Jen did as Kate told her to, and Kate inched forward to kneel down in the dirt beside the young girl, Ashley right behind her. As soon as Ashley was beside her, Jen grabbed her mother's hand and held it tightly.

"I'm okay, Mum," Jen said bravely. "My leg hurts, but I don't think it's broken. I just can't get it out. Did Josh find you?" Her voice trembled slightly at the end.

"Yes, he's waiting outside."

Ashley hugged her daughter.

"Let me have the light so I can see what's got you caught." Kate took the flashlight from the young girl and shone it all around, running the light over the ceiling and walls to see if there was any danger from more cave-ins. Everything looked stable, and the section that had fallen seemed to have come from the wall rather than the roof of the mine shaft.

Jen was on her side, her legs twisted under a large

wooden beam that lay across her ankles. Kate handed the flashlight to Ashley and then gave the beam a shove. It rocked slightly but didn't budge.

"The wood's not pushing on my legs very hard," Jen said helpfully. "I got Josh to try to take my sneakers off, but he couldn't reach them."

"No. I can see there're some smaller pieces of wood under this beam. They've got you caught, but having this heavier support beam resting on your legs probably saved you."

There was no way Kate could see that they could free Jen without moving the weighty strut. Kate evaluated the situation. If they couldn't lift it, they could try levering it with the tire iron. If that failed, they'd have to go for help.

"If Jen holds the light and shines it over toward the beam, do you think between us we could lift it together?" Ashley asked, her voice strained.

"We'll have a go," Kate said, and Ashley handed the light back to her daughter.

Jen turned it until the light shone on the rotting timber, which to Kate was looking heavier by the minute. She couldn't see Ashley's face, so she didn't know how confident she was feeling. "Are you mad at me, Mum?" Jenny asked tremulously, and Ashley wiped her daughter's hair back from her grimy face.

"I was just worried about you. Now, don't try moving unless we tell you to. Ready, Kate?"

Kate nodded, and after some trouble got her arms under the timber. Ashley followed suit. They counted down and then heaved at the beam. It rocked but didn't budge. After two tries they'd barely moved it.

Kate sat back, catching her breath. They'd have to go for help.

"Can we try pushing it with our legs?" Ashley's voice sounded thin with concern. "If we sit back like this, do you think that would work?"

"It's worth a try." Kate got herself into position beside Ashley, and they pushed out with their legs.

The timber slid a few inches. Moving it a little at a time they eventually got the wood to slip back. Then Jen gave a wriggle, and her feet came free.

"I'm out," she cried eagerly, and Ashley clutched her daughter to her.

Kate rescued the flashlight from the floor where Jen had dropped it. The dark cavern was starting to close in on her, and she began to think again of further cave-ins. "Let's go then," she said as casually as she could. "Think you can walk, Jen?"

With her mother's and Kate's help, Jen struggled to her feet. Kate shone the light toward the opening, and they half carried Jen out into the daylight.

Josh seemed to slump his tensed muscles as they appeared. "Is she okay?" he asked anxiously, and Jen grinned.

"I'm okay, just my right ankle's pretty sore."

Kate's gaze met Ashley's, relief reflected in her eyes, and she tried to smile.

"Perhaps Jen shouldn't walk too much until we get a doctor to look at her leg," Kate suggested. Ashley nodded.

"Kate and I will link our arms and make a seat for you to sit on," Ashley told Jen, and they supported her down to the fence.

Josh helped hold the barbed wire aside, and soon they were back at the car. By the time the doctors and nurses at the casualty department of the local hospital had cleaned and dressed both children's cuts and scratches and verified with X rays that nothing was broken, it was almost eight o'clock. Kate drove them all home, and while Ashley supervised baths Kate made hamburgers out of leftovers from the party the night before.

She opened the refrigerator to replace the unused salads when she spied a scrap of paper sticking out from under the fridge. She reached down to pick it up and realized she was holding the note Jenny and Josh had insisted they'd left for Ashley. It must have blown onto the floor while Ashley slept.

"Well, that solves that mystery," Ashley said when they returned to the kitchen and Kate showed her the note.

"I told you we'd left the note, Mum," Jen reiterated. "I'd never go anywhere without telling you first."

Ashley gave her a squeeze. "I know. That's why I was so worried about you both when I discovered you'd gone."

"Next time I'll put a rock on the note," Jenny said.

"Next time you'd better wake me up, hmm?" Ashley advised her. "Just to be on the safe side."

Jenny nodded. "Okay," she said with a sigh. "But you were so tired."

Kate caught Ashley's quick glance at her and felt her face flush. She set the hamburgers on plates and passed them around. The four of them ate ravenously.

"You and Mum should have a shower, too," Jen said after they'd eaten. She was somewhat subdued after the discussion they'd had about the dangerous side of what she referred to as adventures. "You're all dusty and grimy as well."

Ashley looked across at Kate. "Why don't you go in and have a shower while Jenny and Josh help me stack the dishwasher."

"I can shower when I get home. You get cleaned up, and I'll do the clearing away," Kate suggested, loath to leave Ashley but feeling obliged to make an effort not to appear too eager to stay.

Yet that's exactly what Kate wanted to do. She wanted to help Ashley into bed, tuck her in, kiss her good night. Make love to her again. And again. But she knew she was being selfish. Ashley still looked tired and drawn. She'd been through a stressful afternoon and evening.

"Actually, I'd like to talk to you, Kate," Ashley said carefully and glanced at the attentive children. "About the author afternoon at the library," she fabricated a little breathlessly.

Her cheeks flamed, and Kate swallowed, knowing Ashley was thinking about last night. In those few seconds Kate tortured herself with different scenarios.

What would Ashley say about it? Did she still feel the same or would she have changed her mind again? What if she now felt she'd got Kate out of her system as Rosemary suggested Kate should do? And what did Kate herself want?

Silly question, her inner voice jeered. *Or no question at all.* Kate knew she wanted Ashley as she always had. Only more so.

And then she recalled that moment last night when Jen had been about to go to bed. Kate had known then how much she cared about Ashley. And her daughter.

"The author afternoon," she repeated, trying to keep her voice even, also aware of the children listening. "Oh. All right. Perhaps I could go home and shower and change and maybe come back for an hour or so."

Ashley looked as though she would argue and then she nodded. "That would be great."

She refused Kate's offer of help with the dinner dishes, so Kate set off home, complete with a borrowed flashlight to light her way.

Had it only been short hours ago that she'd trod this same path with Ashley, walked beside her up the steps and into the house? And ended up making such exhilarating love with her.

And it had been exhilarating, Kate admitted. Her memories of making love with Ashley had been wonderful, but last night had been indescribable. Kate's body had responded as though, all these years, it had been lying dormant, poised, waiting for Ashley to touch her again.

Kate paused beneath the tamarind tree and looked up at their hideaway. The heat of the day still hovered in the air, a desultory breeze barely shimmering the fine leaves on the old tree, shadowy against the night sky.

Here she and Ashley had laughed and cried, told secrets and made plans, kissed and made love. And here they'd had their one and only full-scale argument. Well, the argument had started here in the tree house, but they'd finished it at the football club dance.

Kate remembered how bad she'd felt afterward, dying a thousand deaths during the week of silence when they didn't so much as look at each other. And just when Kate could stand it no longer, was preparing to go over to the Macleans' and talk to Ashley, Ashley had called her. Ashley's family was out, so Kate slipped through the fence and they'd apologized, held each other, and made love.

She could see them now, sitting in their leafy retreat all those years ago. She remembered so vividly the feeling of dread that had swept over her when Ashley casually stated that Dean had asked her to go to the dance with him.

"You aren't going, are you?" she asked tremulously, and Ashley shrugged.

"Why not? Maybe it'll be fun."

"Oh, Ash, no. Don't go with him." The entreaty burst from Kate before she could hold back the words.

"It'll be all right, Kate. You'll go too, with Phillip. Dean said Phillip's going to ask you to."

"I don't want to go with Phillip. I won't be able to stand dancing with him," Kate said miserably. And she knew what she wanted to say was that she wouldn't be able to endure seeing Ashley dancing with Dean Andrews.

"You don't have to dance every dance with Phillip. Besides, Tim says the dances are great. They play mostly modern music so we wouldn't have to do any cheek to cheek stuff."

"Oh, sure."

"Kate, everyone expects us to go with Dean and Phillip," Ashley said earnestly, and Kate bit her lip.

"Who is this everyone, anyway?" Kate demanded petulantly.

"Well, my parents. Friends. Everyone at school."

"This is getting far too involved, Ash. Don't you see that?" Kate appealed. "Surely we don't have to go with them all the time? Next thing you know this same everyone will be saying we're going steady with Dean and Phillip. And I'd hate that."

Ashley clasped her arms around her legs and rested her chin on her knees. She was silent for a while, and then she sighed.

"Kate, I like it that Mum and Dad think I'm going out with Dean. And it has put an end to Tim's awful insinuations."

The sinking feeling in Kate's stomach grew more insistent, and she swallowed. "I just wish the year was over and we were down in Brisbane together."

"We will be." Ashley smiled and ran her fingers slowly along Kate's cheek, resting her fingertips on Kate's lips. Then she kissed her. "And, apart from that, I can cope with Mum's mother-daughter talks about what not to do with boys far better than I could cope if she started on what I should and shouldn't do with you."

Kate laughed in spite of the bad feelings she had about the upcoming dance. She slid her hands under Ashley's shirt and teased her hardening nipples. "Shall we do what we shouldn't?"

The pleasure of making love forced Kate's disquiet from her mind, but as the day of the dance drew closer she felt a renewed apprehension. Phillip was borrowing his mother's car, and Ashley was going in Dean's car. To Kate this only seemed to force her further away from Ashley.

And for Kate the dance had been as stressful as she predicted it would be.

Quite a few of their classmates were there with partners and, in the beginning, the women had seated themselves at one end of the hall while the men clustered around the beer keg at the opposite end.

This wasn't so bad, Kate decided, and began to relax a little even though the music was so loud she suspected she'd end up with a king-size headache. At least no one was dancing so she could sit with Ashley and a couple of their friends from school.

The others were telling Ashley who they'd come with to the dance and giggling over who had paired with whom.

"Wow, Ash!" one of the young women exclaimed excitedly. "Dean Andrews is gorgeous. You're so lucky to be going out with him. We'd all just die if he'd asked us."

"You probably would die, Joanie," said Wendy, the class comedian. "Ashley would see to it, wouldn't you, Ash?"

Ashley laughed, her color high.

Kate's heart sank. She fought the urge to pull Ashley to her, tell everyone this thing with Dean Andrews was all a sham, that she, Kate Ballantyne, was the one Ashley really loved.

"Dean's so cool," said another girl. "Oh, good grief! He's coming this way."

Kate turned and watched as Dean approached. She felt her jaw tense. He joined their group with the easy confidence of someone who knew he was admired.

"Want to dance, Ash?" he asked, taking her hand and pulling her to her feet. He slid his arm around her waist, leading her onto the dance floor without waiting for her acquiescence.

Kate fumed inwardly as the other young women gazed at the couple with envy.

"Don't they look so romantic together," someone said, and Kate had to close her eyes as a shaft of jealousy sliced through her like a knife.

Gradually the others joined the dancers on the floor, and Kate wished miserably she hadn't let Ashley talk her into coming. Then Phillip materialized beside her and asked her to dance. Reluctantly she stood up and followed him. Anything was better than sitting watching Ashley and Dean together.

Phillip began moving self-consciously to the music, and Kate tried to relax. Neither she nor Phillip looked at each other as they danced. Kate couldn't seem to get with the beat, and she slid a glance at Phillip, deciding he looked as awkward as she felt.

A couple of interminable hours later, Kate could scarcely wait for the evening to end. She'd barely seen or spoken to Ashley, who had danced most of the night with Dean while Kate tried to pretend to Phillip she was enjoying herself. To Kate it felt as though the evening was going to go on forever.

And then the lights dimmed and the band struck up a slow, schmaltzy number. To Kate's horror, Phillip stepped up to Kate and pulled her into his arms. She tried desperately to hide the distaste she felt when his damp palm clutched at hers.

It took all her concentration to hold herself apart from him, and then she saw Ashley and Dean, their bodies molded together. As Kate watched, Dean bent his head and began kissing Ashley. And Ashley didn't try to pull away. As far as Kate could see, Ashley was kissing him back.

Kate stumbled in her agitation, and Phillip took

advantage of it to propel Kate up against him. She cringed, her face flaming in the semidarkness as she felt the hardness of his erection against her stomach.

As the song ended, Kate broke away from him, mumbling about having to go to the rest room, and she hurried through the jam of other dancers.

Safely inside the rest room, Kate drew a steadying breath. Two women had just finished repairing their makeup and left as Kate splashed her burning face with cool water. She was just drying her hands on a paper towel when Ashley appeared beside her.

"Phew! Isn't it hot?" She slid a sideways glance at Kate and looked quickly away. "I saw you dancing with Phillip. Having a good time?"

"You have to be joking, Ash." Kate leaned tiredly against the wash basin.

"Well, you don't have to dance with him. Just enjoy yourself."

"Like you're doing?" Kate asked sharply, and Ashley turned to the towel dispenser.

"Well, yes." Ashley glanced nervously at the toilet cubicles, assuring herself they were alone.

"Do you have to be all over him?" Kate whispered urgently.

"We were just dancing."

"You couldn't have got any closer to him if you'd tried, and I saw you kissing him." Kate's voice broke in a mixture of anger and dejection.

"A kiss is nothing," Ashley said quickly. "It doesn't mean anything."

"Does it also mean nothing when you kiss me?" Kate asked, and Ashley looked around.

"Don't, Kate. Look, we can't talk here."

"I knew we shouldn't have come to this wretched dance," Kate cried angrily.

Ashley sighed. "I told you it's what's expected of us," she said tiredly, and Kate glared at her.

"Camouflage, you mean?" Kate said caustically and then appealed to the other girl. "Ash, I hate all this."

"So do I." Ashley placated. "But it's only a dance."

Kate looked at her suspiciously. "Are you sure you aren't enjoying all this stuff?"

Ashley shook her head. "I enjoy being with you," she said softly. "We just have to —"

"Pretend. I know. I know." Kate looked across at Ashley, and suddenly she shivered. "Ash, I'm worried. About Dean. He's getting serious about you. He —" She swallowed, unsure whether she should tell Ashley what Dean had said at the movies. "He wants to marry you," she blurted out.

Ashley's expression barely changed, and Kate looked at her in surprise. "You know?" she asked, and Ashley nodded.

"He mentioned it."

"What did you say?"

Ashley paused. "I said maybe. But that I was too young to be thinking of marriage."

"Oh, Ash." Kate felt as though she'd been stabbed in the chest.

"You know we have to be careful."

"Not so careful you have to get married," Kate burst out.

"Stop worrying. I'm too young to tie myself down."

"Belinda was only eighteen when she married Mark," Kate reminded her, and Ashley shrugged.

"That was Belinda. Mum probably thought she'd

get pregnant if she didn't let her get married." She smoothed her dress. "Come on, Kate. Stop worrying. We're doing the foursome thing, Dean and me and you and Phillip. Where's the problem in that?"

"Except there hasn't been four of us tonight. We've been two sets of two." Kate bit her lip. "I want it to be just us, Ashley."

Ashley drew in a deep breath. "Well, it can't be, Kate. We have to protect our reputations. And that means going out with guys. That's how it has to be."

"It's living a lie," Kate began, and Ashley paced angrily across the small room.

"Lie or not, Kate, I want to be normal. I don't want people looking at me and snickering behind my back. Or calling me dreadful names. Now, I don't want to discuss this any more. I'm going back to the dance."

"Ash —" Kate appealed but Ashley had gone.

And not long after, Kate had pleaded a headache and insisted that Phillip take her home. When he pulled up outside her gate, she had jumped from the car, thanking him as she hurried up the path toward home and the sanctuary of her room.

Kate sighed. Had she been too intense back then? Had her jealousy and possessiveness pushed Ashley further away? Well, she knew she couldn't change the past now. But what about the future?

With one final, rueful look up at the tree house, she continued up the stairs and into her house. She went through to the bathroom and stripped off her dirty shorts and shirt, stepping under the shower.

Now, ten years on, could she blame Ashley for thinking the way she did? It took tremendous courage to stand up in the face of the so-called moral majority. Kate hadn't exactly done it herself, so could she judge Ashley for not being more fearless when they were both so young?

Kate sighed. Would she have been able to face the town back then if they had come out together? Recalling the way she'd reacted when Ashley's mother had discovered them together, Kate rather thought she wouldn't.

She dried herself and slipped into fresh shorts and a cool tank top.

It was getting late, so she'd have to go back. Ashley was expecting her to. She retraced her steps through the fence. The pool twinkled in the moonlight, reflections forever changing.

Ashley was waiting for her at the door and slid the screen open for Kate to enter. She looked at Kate a little uncertainly and ran her tongue tip nervously over her lips.

Kate watched her do this, couldn't seem to draw her eyes away from Ashley's mouth, her full lips. The memory of those lips moving over her filled her, wrapped itself about her like a warm rug on a cold evening, and Kate shivered slightly.

"The kids are sound asleep. Thanks for coming back over, Kate," Ashley said softly, and Kate dragged her eyes from Ashley's mouth to gaze into her eyes.

Then she found herself drowning in their blue depths, indigo now as Ashley stood backlit by the mood lights she'd switched on over by the sofa. Kate also noticed the dark smudges of tiredness under

Ashley's eyes and knew the other woman was totally worn-out.

"Perhaps we should have left this until tomorrow. You look exhausted."

Ashley gave a crooked smile. "Are you trying to tell me I don't look my best?"

"You look beautiful," Kate said softly, and tears gathered on Ashley's eyelashes, one trickling down her cheek.

Stepping forward, Kate slid her arms around Ashley's waist and let Ashley lean into her. A sob caught in Ashley's throat.

"I thought I'd lost Jen today," she said thickly. "I couldn't have borne that. She's the only good thing to come out of the disaster that was Dean and me."

Kate gently brushed a strand of Ashley's hair back from her forehead. "Let's sit down."

They moved over to the sofa they'd sat on so decorously the evening before. Only this time they strained together, bodies touching, and Ashley took Kate's hand.

"I don't know what I'd have done today without you, Kate. If you hadn't been home ... Thank you."

Kate shrugged. "I was about to come over here to see you anyway."

"Were you?" Ashley bit her lip, and Kate took a steadying breath.

"I couldn't keep away any longer." There. She'd said it.

The air about them seemed to be suspended, motionless, holding time captured. And then Ashley let her head rest back against the couch. She closed her eyes, and suddenly she was crying again.

Kate turned to her, frowning in concern. "Ash, please. Don't cry. I didn't mean to pressure you. If you don't want to ... If you've changed your mind ..."

Ashley sat up, releasing Kate's hand to cup Kate's face in her palms. "Changed my mind?" She shook her head, smiling through her tears. "No way, my darling Kate. I made a mistake by letting you go ten years ago. I'm not making the same mistake twice." She leaned forward and tenderly kissed Kate's lips, her touch as soft as a feather, lingering exquisitely.

Kate melted into her. They clung together until their kisses deepened, long, drugging, desperate kisses that left them both breathless.

Taking Kate's hand, Ashley touched her lips to each fingertip, then pressed her mouth to Kate's palm. "Say you love me, Kate. Like I love you. I need so much to hear you say it."

"I love you, Ashley. I always have," Kate said simply, and Ashley sighed.

"I despaired of ever hearing you say that again. We've wasted ten long years, and it's all my fault. I'm so sorry, Kate. Can you forgive me?"

"Let's put the past behind us, go on from here. No recriminations."

"I shouldn't have allowed myself to be manipulated into marrying Dean. I was such a coward." She shook her head. "I have so much to apologize for."

"Ash, don't —" Kate began, but Ashley touched a finger to her lips.

"No. Let me explain, Kate. I need to."

Kate nodded reluctantly.

"Remember the football club dance?"

Kate nodded again. "Yes, I remember."

A flash of pain passed over Ashley's face, and she sighed. "That was the start of it all. I can't believe I was so horrible to you, Kate. I was just so mixed up. I was trying to prove to myself that I could be like everyone else, and I hurt you badly. I hurt us both. Letting Dean kiss me at the dance was part of it. I wanted to . . . I wanted kissing him to be as wonderful as kissing you. And I was angry because it wasn't."

She looked away, her fingers playing absently with Kate's. "Then you and I had that argument and I stalked off because I knew all you'd said was true. And then you left. If I'd —" She stopped. "Dean insisted on taking me parking on the way home. I thought it was expected, another way to prove myself. Did you go parking with Phillip?"

Kate shook her head. "No."

"No," Ashley repeated softly. "I didn't think you would have. You were always more sensible than I was. Well, Dean started kissing me, and I tried to like it. But he wasn't you, Kate. By the time I realized what a fool I was, things had got out of hand. I tried to tell him I'd changed my mind but he thought I was just playing hard to get. At least that's what he said."

"He raped you?" Kate whispered, horrified, and Ashley gave a self-disparaging laugh.

"Technically I suppose he did, but I wasn't blameless. I allowed him to think, well, you know, and then I panicked. It was pretty awful. Afterward he apologized."

"Oh, Ash."

"Every time Dean rang me, my mother beamed. The boys kept saying he was a good bloke. But all I wanted was you, Kate. And yet every way I turned, everyone, everything pointed to it being so wrong.

Mum. Pastor Jones. All the jokes directed at Maggie and Georgie. I was so confused.

"Then I missed my period. I was terrified, Kate. I wanted to tell you, but I thought you'd hate me. It was from that night of the dance. That was the only time we did it. Dean wore a condom, but it came off or something when we were struggling. It was a complete fiasco.

"I went to the doctor, and he confirmed it. I was so scared, Kate. I was trying to tell you that afternoon when Mum walked in on us. After you left, Mum and I had a huge argument, and I told her I was pregnant and that I was going away with you.

"That's when Mum pulled out all the stops. She forbade me to see you. Dad was sent off to talk to Dean, and Mum booked the church. I was in shock I think, because before I knew it I was married. I let everyone drag me along. I took the path of least resistance. It was easier that way."

"If only you'd told me, Ash," Kate said, her chest tight with unshed tears.

"Looking back I felt as though it was all happening to someone else, that I was simply watching on. Even when I was saying 'I do' I expected you to come charging in to carry me off."

"I was in the tree house waiting for you. Fine knight in shining armor I was," Kate added lightly, and they both tried to laugh.

"The first few months of our marriage was pure hell. Every time Dean touched me I'd throw up, probably a mixture of my pregnancy and nerves. So I borrowed money and came home looking for you.

"I begged Mum and Dad to let me stay with them,

but they said I hadn't given my marriage long enough. And I couldn't find you in Brisbane.

"After Jen was born, Dean was a little more considerate for a while. But then he started to get possessive again, and I came home again. And as you know I went back. But I'll never do that again. I'm in control of my own life now, Kate, and I know what I want."

She looked across at Kate and held her gaze. "I love you, Kate. And I want to be with you. But if you don't want us to live together I'll accept that. I mean, I don't know how you'd feel about Jen being with us. I just want to be near you. To be part of your life. What" — she swallowed — "what do you want, Kate?"

"What I've always wanted, Ash. You. And Jen's part of you. How could I not love her too? She's so much like you." Kate ran her fingertip along the curve of Ashley's cheek. "I love you so much. These ten years I've felt as though I'd lost part of me. I need you, Ash, to make me whole."

They kissed deeply, urgently whispering their love for each other, until eventually they drew back, smiling tiredly.

"I can't understand why I didn't just race you off when you first came home," Kate said teasingly. "I was such a fool."

Ashley laughed and then sobered. "I thought I'd left coming home too late. Thoughts of you were all that kept me going when things got unbearable."

"Why didn't you write to me? Aunt Jane would have sent on your letter."

"I'm not so sure she would have, Kate. I don't think she ever approved of me somehow. But apart from that, I didn't dare write. Dean was . . . his temper was terrifying. If he'd found out how I felt about you, I don't know what he'd have done to me or to you. There was a dark side to him.

"But I got my life sorted out and started writing." She looked at Kate. "And I really did write *Gold Fever* as a tribute to us, Kate."

"It's a wonderful book, Ash. I just . . ." Kate paused. "With you arriving home and the turmoil that threw me into, well, I guess the way Clare and Tess were with each other, the tender poignancy of it, struck a raw nerve. It brought back all the pain I felt losing you and . . ." Kate shrugged.

"I really messed things up, didn't I?" Ashley said softly, and Kate sighed.

"We were just kids, Ash. We weren't really equipped to handle the intensity of it all. I know now I wasn't."

"I guess not. But I wish it had been different." Ashley looked at Kate with a frown of concern. "Do you think we *can* put it all behind us, Kate?" she asked, her gaze not wavering from Kate's.

Kate leaned forward and kissed her gently. "I think we can," she said sincerely.

Ashley gave a tentative smile. "I'm just so glad —" Her lips trembled and she swallowed. "When I came in search of you, I don't think I allowed myself to picture past actually getting here. Then, that first day, when I came over to see you, and your friend Rosemary walked in, I was sure I was too late.

"The way she was with you, the way she looked at you, the subtle togetherness. I was so burningly jealous of her I couldn't stop myself trying to warn her off."

"I guess I treated Rosemary badly," Kate said slowly. "We were friends, had been for some time, and then we" — Kate grimaced — "I allowed it to go further when I shouldn't have. I wasn't free to get involved with anyone. I never have been. You were always with me, Ash."

Ashley squeezed her hand, and Kate laughed softly.

"When I was staying in Rob's house in Brisbane, two women moved in when the first couple got married. I had an affair with one of them, trying to prove I was over you." Kate rolled her eyes. "She always said she felt as though when she kissed me there was someone else there with us. She wasn't far wrong."

"You've always been in my heart too, Kate. I never stopped loving you." She kissed Kate again and murmured appreciatively.

"Ash." Kate held her away and looked into her eyes. "Things haven't changed that much. Your mother may still feel the same about us. And then there's your family."

Ashley nodded. "I know. But we'll weather that, Kate. I'm not allowing anyone else to come between us again."

"What about Jen?" Kate asked.

"Jen knows how much I care about you. I've told her. We'll tell her together that we love each other and want to be a family."

"Will she understand?" Kate persisted.

"She knows what a lesbian is, Kate. Kids these days are pretty well-informed compared to how we were at their age. Apart from that she heard Dean making a derisive remark about two gay women and asked me about it later. I explained, and she frowned and told me her father was wrong to say awful things about people he didn't know. I know I'm prejudiced, Kate, but Jen is a very well-adjusted young person. And she loves you already. You were, after all, my partner in all my adventure stories."

Kate raised her eyebrows, and Ashley pulled a face. "I know. Look where all my stories led. Perhaps in future I'll have to add an appendix to each story, reiterating that she not try out each escapade."

Kate laughed. "Perhaps that might be best."

"So." Ashley nibbled Kate's earlobe. "Shall we pick up where we left off ten years ago?"

"What *do* you mean?" Kate feigned puzzlement.

"Shall we continue to have adventures, you and I?" Ashley explained with the light of awareness in her blue eyes.

Kate felt a familiar sensation begin to build inside her. "Do you have any particular adventures in mind?"

"Oh, I can think of any number of adventures. Strange thing is, though, these adventures all seem to have one common denominator. Their very erotic contents. What do you think that means?"

Kate made a show of giving the question serious thought. "I suspect it means we're both on the very same, most delightful wavelength."

Ashley laughed softly. "Then nothing's changed, my darling Kate. We always were," she said as she turned her lips to Kate's and proceeded to prove her point.